"Your offer is g̲___ Susannah."

Trent shook his head. "But money isn't what I want." He angled her even closer, close enough to feel the heat that throbbed through him. "You know what I want."

"But what you want—you can't... What about the paper?" She seemed to be struggling to catch a breath. "You won't...sign it?"

"No, I won't sign it, Sue, but there are other ways."

"Other ways to...what?"

Her lips were half-open, peach-pink, wet and glimmering in the sunlight. And he remembered exactly how they had tasted. How they had felt, on him, around him. For eleven long years, even in dreams, he had been haunted by the memory of their warmth, their hidden strength....

She might hate him, but he had to have this. He refused to go on burning and wanting, and being forever denied. Though she wouldn't admit it, she burned, too.

"Trent. Tell me what you mean."

He let his body answer her.

Dear Reader,

For those of you who read *Texas Baby* and saw the sparks between Trent Maxwell and Susannah Everly, it won't be a surprise to learn that I struggled to find a happy ending for this star-crossed couple.

They have such an emotional history...years of love, followed by years of bitterness. They've spent a decade denying their deepest feelings. How on earth could I move them toward truce, forgiveness and, finally, back to love?

Sometimes it seemed impossible. One thing kept me searching: the letters and e-mails I got from readers, asking for Trent and Susannah's story. Those eager notes reminded me that we all want to see love triumph over anger and pain.

We don't just want it. We *need* it.

All our relationships face challenges. Somehow we must have faith that we can rise above our failures. We must hang on to the hope that we can forgive, and be forgiven.

So to all my wonderful readers, thanks for the inspiration—and for waiting. I hope you enjoy watching these two find love again. And please stay in touch. Visit me at KOBrienonline.com, or write me at KOBrien@aol.com. Your messages mean more than you'll ever know!

Warmly,

Kathleen O'Brien

TEXAS WEDDING
Kathleen O'Brien

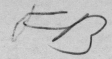

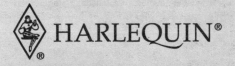

HARLEQUIN®

TORONTO • NEW YORK • LONDON
AMSTERDAM • PARIS • SYDNEY • HAMBURG
STOCKHOLM • ATHENS • TOKYO • MILAN • MADRID
PRAGUE • WARSAW • BUDAPEST • AUCKLAND

Recycling programs
for this product may
not exist in your area.

ISBN-13: 978-0-373-71572-5

TEXAS WEDDING

Copyright © 2009 by Kathleen O'Brien.

www.eHarlequin.com

Printed in U.S.A.

ABOUT THE AUTHOR

Kathleen O'Brien was a feature writer and TV critic before marrying a fellow journalist. Motherhood, which followed soon after, was so marvelous she turned to writing novels, which could be done at home. She's an unapologetic sentimentalist, with an iPod full of corny music, a den full of three-hanky romances and an address book full of lifelong friends. She loves reading in her backyard bower, though she struggles to keep even the ferns alive, and could never, ever manage a thousand acres of peaches!

Don't miss any of our special offers. Write to us at the following address for information on our newest releases.

Harlequin Reader Service
U.S.: 3010 Walden Ave., P.O. Box 1325, Buffalo, NY 14269
Canadian: P.O. Box 609, Fort Erie, Ont. L2A 5X3

CHAPTER ONE

SUSANNAH EVERLY MAXWELL had been hiding in the bathroom for half an hour. For a bride on her wedding night, that was at least twenty-nine minutes too long.

She'd left the shower on, hoping Trent would assume she was still bathing, and the cascade of warm water had turned the room into a sauna. The towel knotted at her breasts hung heavily, saturated with moisture. Steam smothered the mirror, forming a blank screen of mist.

She knew she should go out into the bedroom, where her new husband was waiting, but she couldn't force herself to do it.

Her new husband…

None of this seemed real. Reaching out one fingertip, she began to write on the glass.

Mrs…. Trent… Maxwell…

She'd penned the name a thousand times, in the turquoise ink she'd loved back in high school. But before she could finish the last syllable, the condensation pooled and began to run. It was like trying to write with tears.

Her reflection appeared in the open spaces, fractured into a collection of mismatched parts. Ironically, this stranger draped in the white towel, wreathed in clouds

of steam, looked more like a bride than she had this afternoon at the courthouse.

But not a happy bride. A broken Picasso bride, or maybe a ghost bride from some terrifying urban legend—a
confused wraith who would never find her way out of
the mist.

She touched her damp cheek, as if she needed to
confirm that she was made of solid flesh. Her new
diamond ring sparkled in the mirror.

After all this time, she was really Trent Maxwell's
wife. For one year, anyhow. Not exactly the "forever"
she used to dream of.

Suddenly, hard knuckles rapped against wood.

"Susannah?"

Staring at the door, she put her left hand against her
heart, which once again thump-jogged in place.

Stop that, she commanded it. But her heart ignored her.

"Susannah? Are you all right?"

He didn't turn the knob. He probably knew it was
locked. Not that the flimsy button would have kept him
out if he'd really wanted to come in. And he would
come in, sooner or later, if she didn't emerge. The Fates
had blessed Trent Maxwell with a lot of gifts, but
patience wasn't one of them.

She'd fallen for Trent when she was just a kid—not
all that much younger than her little sister Nikki was now.
Susannah had thought she was so grown-up, ready to be
in love. Now, watching Nikki struggle with hormones at
the oh-so-mature age of sixteen, she knew better.

It had all been dreams. She'd fantasized about standing
at the altar beside him. She'd dreamed of cooking him

spaghetti and darning his socks, though she had no clue what that meant.

But those dreams had gone up in flames—quite literally—eleven years ago. Since then, she and Trent had barely exchanged fifty civil words.

Now here she was, a thirty-year-old woman, embarking on a one-year marriage of convenience. How dry those words sounded! They didn't capture any of the heart-skittering anticipation. He was only ten yards away, and waiting for her to come to bed. This would be a real marriage, he'd insisted. And, because she needed a husband, she had agreed.

But maybe she wasn't trapped. She had one last hope—a piece of paper hidden in her nightstand that somehow might miraculously save her.

She tried to imagine handing it to him. Tried to visualize his face as he read it. What would he say? They'd been so close once that they could finish each other's sentences. But the bitter years lay between them now like a continent of ice. Her new husband was a stranger to her, and she had no idea how he would react.

"Susannah?"

His voice wasn't angry. Not yet. That would come later. Later, when he read the paper. When he found out what her plans were for this, the first of their 365 nights of married life.

Her gaze returned to the pieces of woman reflected between the finger-written letters. *Mrs*... Her eyes shone. *Trent*... Her lips were parted, vulnerable.

Who *was* that woman? Suddenly horrified, she drew her eyebrows together. That woman looked like a victim.

Ridiculous. No one had abducted her, tricked her or sold her into wedlock. The bargain had been her idea, the only sensible escape from an impossible situation. It was just that marriage to Trent had seemed so much more manageable when it was weeks, days, even hours in the future, instead of right here, right now.

But she could handle it. She wasn't weak. Ask anyone, from the lowliest fruit picker on her payroll to the richest buyer on the market. You could even ask her grandfather's ghost, which was probably still prowling the halls of Hell, carrying his favorite switching strap.

They'd all tell you. Susannah Everly faced her problems. She took her medicine. And she did it with her chin held high.

"I'm coming."

She reached in and punched off the shower. *Enough.* She wasn't weak.

She unknotted the towel and let it slide to the ground. Then she plucked her gray, shapeless nightgown from the counter and tugged it over her head.

Hideous.

Perfect.

She wrapped her fingers around the warm doorknob and twisted.

Showtime.

"I'm sorry, Trent. I…"

Her voice dwindled off. The silent shadows of the bedroom momentarily disoriented her. Was he gone? Instead of the hot voice she'd expected to hear accosting her, demanding an explanation, she was met only by quiet currents of dark air and the faint smell of roses.

That must mean Trent had opened the east window—the roses had climbed as far as the second-story sill this spring and seemed to be trying to nudge the glass open with their pink-and-yellow faces.

She took a deep breath. She adored those flowers, just as she cherished every inch of Everly. She mustn't forget that. She might have grown to hate Trent, but she'd never stopped loving this beautiful ranch, set like a jewel in the middle of a thousand acres of peach orchards.

She was doing this to save Everly.

As her eyes adjusted, she finally saw Trent. He leaned against the window frame with his back angled to her, staring down into the side yard, though she knew he couldn't see much except the grapevine trellis that covered the wicker patio loungers.

Half his body was in shadow. He wore no shirt. Moonlight turned one muscular shoulder and arm to marble, then glimmered against the silver tip of his belt buckle before being swallowed up by the black of his pants.

Her heart tried once again to escape, but she squared her shoulders and forced it into submission. She had made promises. Maybe he'd let her out of them, and maybe he wouldn't. Either way, this had to be faced.

"Trent?"

He tilted his head toward her. "Well, hello," he said with a smile that just caught the moonlight. "I was beginning to wonder if you'd climbed out the bathroom window."

"No." She tried to match his sardonic tone, and she was glad that he probably couldn't see her flush. "Of course not. Don't be silly."

"You think it's silly?" He moved toward her with a lazy confidence, as if he knew he had all the time in the world. As if he owned this night. As if he owned *her*, which, in a way, he did.

"Why silly? Are you trying to tell me you've really been in the shower all this time?"

She'd never been a good liar. The only person she'd ever needed to lie to had been her grandfather, and her pride had forced her to battle it out with him, toe-to-toe, instead. So now she hesitated just a moment too long.

Trent reached her just as she was opening her mouth to say *yes, yes, of course I've been in the shower.*

One eyebrow rose in that classic, mocking arch as he shook his head slowly. He laid his finger against her lips.

"No," he said. "Don't bother to fib. If you'd been under water all this time, you'd be as wrinkled as a raisin."

Instinctively, she folded her hands into fists. He glanced down at them, and his grin deepened. "Shall we look?"

Damn him…he was so cool, so amused by her discomfort. When he touched her hand, she had to resist the urge to slap him. He hadn't bought the right to mock her.

But he *had* bought the right to touch her. He'd been very clear about that. No way in hell was he going to sign on for a year of chastity. "I'm no saint," he had said, with that maddening smile that made it impossible to tell how he really felt. "So you'd better decide whether you can deal with sharing my bed for a whole year."

He took one of her hands, gently pried open the

fingers and held it up for inspection. Her fingers were warm and damp, but smooth. No wrinkles. She'd been in the shower a total of maybe five minutes, just long enough to scrub off her makeup.

"So what *were* you doing in there?" His gaze flicked across her wet hair and bare face, then skimmed the lumpy contours of her overwashed nightgown. "Not primping, apparently. Although…it might have taken a while to dig up anything as unflattering as this rag."

"If I'd had enough money to buy a trousseau, Trent, I wouldn't have needed a husband in the first place."

He chuckled. Could this really be funny to him? Surely he, too, remembered how often they had dreamed of their wedding night. That fairy-tale dream had sparkled with magic, with lace and music and romance and roses. The reality was going to be so different….

But perhaps the fairy dust had been her dream, not his. Though they'd been close, she hadn't ever completely understood him, with his cryptic smiles and his elegant indifference. Perhaps, for him, it had just been about the sex.

"What exactly are you trying to accomplish with all this, Susannah?"

"All what?"

He tugged at the sleeve of her nightgown. The neckline was shot, so even that light pressure caused it to slip over her shoulder. She felt suddenly half-naked.

"This plain-Jane costume. Were you hoping it would turn me off? Did you think you could make yourself so ugly I'd run screaming from the marriage bed?"

"No."

"Good. Because that really would be silly." He set her hand free and put his forefinger under her chin. "The chemistry between us has nothing to do with packaging. It never has."

She couldn't deny it. Back when they were little more than kids, this fire between them had erupted like one of her grandfather's oil drills hitting a pocket of natural gas. Nothing had been strong enough to put it out. It had overpowered pimples and puberty, flus and hangovers, bad moods and bad hair, and even the day the skunk sprayed her right in the face.

It had even outlived love.

She still felt it, arcing between them now. A primal force. Blind and fierce and involuntary.

And dangerous. At least to her.

"Susannah." His voice was a whisper. He moved her wet hair from her shoulder and bent his head toward her bare skin. She made a small, trapped sound, knowing he was going to kiss her.

She couldn't let it happen. Her heart tripped on itself merely at the sound of his voice. The touch of his lips would cause it to explode.

Mumbling something meaningless, she jerked away from him, toward her nightstand. She couldn't breathe, but somehow she kept moving. That piece of paper was her last hope. Like the cyanide pill issued to soldiers, in case of capture.

She flicked on the bedside lamp. Then, her hands shaking only a little, she slid open the top drawer and felt around the stacks of papers inside. It should be on top. She'd written it hastily, only this afternoon.

"I have something…."

She glanced at him, hoping she didn't sound as nervous as she felt. To her surprise, he was smiling. Not a genuine, warm smile, of course—those were rare—but his one-dimple teasing grin was pretty dazzling, too.

"Ah." He glanced at the drawer. "The practical princess strikes again."

"What?" He and Chase had always called her that, back when they were teenagers, and she'd been one inch less reckless than the two boys. But why now? Could he possibly guess what she'd written on that paper?

His dimple deepened. "I think I brought plenty, thanks, though it's nice to know you've got extra. Just in case."

"Extra what?" Then she realized what he meant. Condoms. Her breath came shallowly as she tried not to imagine the tumbled bed, the discarded silver wrappers littering the floor, their sweaty bodies braided together in the moonlight. "No. It's not that. I have something I want to show you."

Finally her fingers closed around the long white envelope. She pulled it out and extended it toward him. "It's something I'd like you to read. Something I'd like you to sign."

He didn't look at the envelope. The smile stayed in place, but it lost any hint of humor. Above it, his gaze held hers, cool and unblinking blue inside a thick fringe of black lashes. Oh, even when he was angry, he was lethally attractive.

"Sign?"

The word was even colder than his eyes.

"Yes," she said, too quickly. "I got to thinking about things, today after the wedding, and I realized we hadn't really considered…everything."

"No? It seemed to me the prenup your lawyer drew up was pretty damn thorough. He made it quite clear that I'll be shot if I'm caught crossing the Everly threshold with so much as one pillowcase from your mother's needlepoint collection." He lifted an eyebrow. "Which wasn't very likely in the first place, was it?"

"No. It was silly, but Richard's careful. He wanted to protect me—"

"Was the medical certificate his idea, too?"

She felt heat crawling up her throat toward her cheeks. The medical certificate had almost scotched the whole deal. But when Trent had insisted on a physical relationship, she had insisted that he prove he was healthy. With his Don Juan past, it would have been insane not to.

"No, that was my idea. Richard doesn't know we— that we agreed to—"

"Consummate the marriage?"

"Right. So when he wrote the prenup, of course he wasn't thinking about…things like that. That's what occurred to me today. That we hadn't provided for every contingency."

She felt foolish, still holding out the envelope. She pushed it a few inches closer, till its crisp edge almost touched his bare, bronze chest, like the tip of a sword.

He glanced down at it dismissively, those long eyelashes dusting his cheeks. "It's a little late to try to glue conditions onto this deal, don't you think?"

Of course it was too late, technically. She knew that. He had the moral right to tear this piece of paper into a dozen pieces and fling it in her face. Many might think he had the moral right to shove her onto the waiting bed and force her to do whatever he wanted.

But surely he wouldn't. Surely even the volcano of anger that had been simmering between them for more than a decade wouldn't blow that high. Surely it hadn't taken the laughing boy who used to dance with her down by Green Fern Pool and turned him into a monster.

"Put it away, Susannah. I'm not signing anything."

She lifted her chin. "Just read it."

She was pleased to note that, though her insides were twisting as if she had a bellyful of snakes, her voice sounded strong. In spite of the hot cheeks and the damp palms, somehow she projected confidence.

She sent a mental thank-you to her grandfather, the bully who had taught her how to face down fear.

Trent tilted his head. "Sue, don't do this," he said. His voice was quiet, but held an undercurrent of warning.

"Please. Just read it."

She saw his chest expand as he took in a deep breath. His rib cage brushed the edge of the envelope.

He reached out, finally, and took it. She hadn't sealed the envelope. She hadn't had time. Chase and Josie, who had no doubt meant well, had brought over a few friends to toast the newlyweds this afternoon, and Susannah had found it difficult to steal away long enough to scrawl the words onto the paper.

Trent unfolded it and began to read.

Her heart thumped in her ears, but not loudly enough to drown out the quavering inner voice that read along with him.

In the event that a child is conceived between me and Susannah Kate Everly during our marriage, I, Trent Anderson Maxwell, do hereby relinquish all legal rights to said child. I will not attempt to gain custody, partial or full, of any child of this union. I will have no financial obligations toward said child, nor will I have any right to be involved in decisions involving the child.

He must have read it three times, his handsome face impassive, his black hair falling over his forehead. At least, that was how many times she could scan it in her head—and each time it sounded more ridiculous, with all that fake legalese mimicking wills and contracts she'd seen over the years.

And each time it sounded more damning. More unfair, and insulting. More like the dishonest swindle it was.

His knuckles were white. So were hers.

Breathe… Though her lungs felt like rusty bellows, she had to remember she needed air. Her head swam, and her ears rang. But she refused to do anything as pathetic as fainting.

Thank God she'd sent Nikki away for the summer. Nikki didn't like Trent and, with the judgmental absolutism of the young, she'd made it clear that she thought the whole marriage-of-convenience idea was disgusting. Knowing it would be impossible to fight on two fronts, Susannah had found the cash for a special art school, managed to wrangle permission to take Nikki out of school a bit early to attend, and, just yesterday, had packed her little sister off.

Barely in the nick of time! Nikki acted tough, especially when she locked horns with Susannah, but it was a facade. No sixteen-year-old was tough enough to handle the hell that might break loose at Everly tonight.

It seemed an eternity before Trent raised his eyes again. When he finally did, the look she saw in them terrified her.

"Tell me this is your idea of a joke."

"Of course it's not." She knew a dignified silence would be more powerful, but she suddenly couldn't seem to stop talking. "It's just common sense. No matter how careful we are, everyone knows that birth control isn't one hundred percent reliable. We can't allow our lives to be tangled up forever, with custody battles and court cases, just because we bought a faulty condom, or because—"

"Don't pretend you're stupid." He held the paper between two fingers, as if he meant to flick it away at any moment. "You know this…this juvenile chicken scratch would never hold up in court."

She raised her chin. "I disagree."

"No, you don't. You know it's absurd. They'd laugh you out of court. But it won't come to that, will it? Because you know damned well I'd never sign any such ridiculous document. *Never.*"

"You have to."

"The hell I do. You made your deal with the devil, Susannah. You can't renegotiate now."

"I can." She met his glacial blue gaze, but it made her shudder inside, as if she'd swallowed a stomachful of chipped ice. "I *am* renegotiating. I have had second thoughts. If you don't sign that document, there will be no…no consummation."

For a minute, he just stared at her. And then, with a sudden oath, he did flick the paper away. He moved toward her, roughly, all six-foot-two-inches of hard, half-naked muscle bearing down.

Every primitive instinct told her to run, but he blocked the way. She backed up on clumsy legs, knocking against the dresser, sending her earrings and wristwatch clanking to the wood floor.

He didn't even seem to hear it. He just kept coming. Finally, she ran out of room, and her shoulder blades met the wall. He slammed the heels of his hands onto the plaster, just inches from each side of her head. His face was so close she could feel the heat of his breath against her cheek.

"This is what you'd planned all along, isn't it? What a fool I was, to think even for a minute that…" He set his jaw into a right angle of fury. "Right from the start, this was just a nasty game of bait and switch."

"No. No, I just realized this afternoon—"

"The hell you did. Don't give me that crap, Susannah. You're not a fool, and neither am I. You never intended to keep your end of the bargain."

She tried to deny it. But she couldn't. Consciously, she'd meant what she said. But somewhere, deep inside, she had always been praying that she wouldn't have to do this.

"Right." He loaded the syllable with disdain. "But did you ever consider the possibility that your game might just backfire on you?"

"No—it wasn't a game—how could it—"

He lowered his lips to her neck and spoke his next words against her skin. "Did it ever occur to you that I might decide not to just slink away with my tail between my legs? That I might decide to claim what's due me?"

"No, that never occurred to me," she lied, swallowing hard. "I trust you to be sensible, and—"

"You *trust* me?" He threw his head back, laughing harshly. "That's a good one, sweetheart. According to that prenup, you don't trust me with the dinner forks. And obviously you didn't trust me not to bring a bucket of STDs to the marriage bed, either."

He bent his elbows slightly, and tilted his body toward her, just close enough that the heat and the pressure reminded her how powerful he was. He'd always been tall, even as a teen, with the promise of potency to come. But this was a man's body, with all the promises fulfilled.

She tried to go numb. She didn't want to feel the angles of his hips against hers. She didn't want to be aware of the muscles in his legs, rippling with tension. She didn't want to remember how this same body had once covered hers with tenderness.

"You obviously believe I'm an immoral bastard—and eleven years ago you told me I was a murderer, too." His rough voice scraped her nerves. "What would stop a man like that from asserting his conjugal rights…with whatever force it required?"

"Nothing." She pressed her head against the wall, struggling to create distance. "You're obviously stronger than I am, Trent. Nothing can stop you except your own conscience."

But did he have one? And what about *her* conscience? She had agreed to a sexual relationship, in exchange for this marriage. If she could anesthetize her conscience, perhaps he could do the same.

For a minute, she thought he might. He let his body press forward even farther, until the granite of his chest met her breasts. His heat scorched through her nightgown. Too fast for her to react, he thrust his knee between her legs and cocked it up, pressing it hard against the aching spot at the apex of her thighs.

She twisted against the wall, trying to escape both him and the hot desire that traitorously shot through her. Perhaps she wasn't strong enough to prevent this, but she could fight. She didn't have to make it easy for him. She pushed against his chest with her palms, but she might as well have been trying to move a mountain.

He let her squirm for a moment, just long enough for her to realize how helpless she truly was. And then, without warning, he stepped away.

If she hadn't been propped up by the wall, she might have fallen. Her breath was coming so fast, it was as if she'd been running for hours.

He, on the other hand, looked as cool and contemptuous as ever. He picked up his shirt and began walking toward the door.

When he put his hand on the knob, he turned.

"It's not my conscience stopping me," he said, looking her over with a cool appraisal that somehow managed to be as insulting as if he'd spit in her face. "It's my standards. I don't much care for liars, or frigid, manipulative bitches. The truth is, sweetheart, you're not worth it."

CHAPTER TWO

YEARS AGO, Trent had learned that there's no frustration, no pain or fury, no mental monster of any kind, that can't be tamed by a treadmill—assuming you go fast enough and stay on it long enough.

This morning, with Susannah's double cross less than twelve hours behind him, he'd logged about ten miles on the gym's machine before he felt even semi-normal. He started Mile One with his cell phone in his hand, fingers itching to call a lawyer, any lawyer, and file for a quickie divorce.

Instead, he dialed up the treadmill speed and jogged till he sweated out some of the poison. Somewhere along the repetitive rubber highway, he found enough sanity to remember why he'd agreed to this marriage in the first place.

It hadn't been just to help Susannah. It hadn't even been just because he'd been fool enough to dream that this might be their second chance.

He'd also done it for Chase.

Originally, Chase had been Susannah's chosen temporary husband. It had made sense. Chase was her best friend. He was unattached and, even more importantly, he was a born saint. The original Mr. DoGood. So he had been perfectly happy to marry her with no demands, no strings attached.

But then Josie Whitford had come along and hit Chase like a bolt of lightning. The poor guy's dilemma had been painful to watch. Love or loyalty? Passion or past promises?

Trent had to say one thing for Susannah: though she was as cold as a meat locker toward Trent, she did seem to have a soft spot for Chase. When she'd realized the problem, she'd come to Trent and laid out a deal.

The way she figured it, Trent should marry her. If he hadn't screwed up their relationship eleven years ago, she said, she wouldn't be in the market for a husband in the first place. So Trent owed her. If he'd help her meet the husband clause in her grandfather's will, she'd consider the debt paid.

Trent knew she was desperate, even to suggest it. He knew she would have exhausted all other options, sane or crazy, before coming to him.

Everyone knew she'd tried to break the will legally, of course. But though old man Everly had been mean as a snake and the biggest male chauvinist in Texas, he'd also been clever and controlling, and he'd apparently found a lawyer who was his match.

The resulting will was apparently ironclad. Arlington had left Everly tied up so tight Susannah couldn't sell a single peach tree, not one pebble on the property, no matter how much she needed money. Not till she got married, and stayed married, sleeping under the same roof with her husband for a full year.

Trent was surprised the will hadn't required a check of the honeymoon bedsheets, to prove all marital obligations had been met. The nasty old bastard.

It had been tempting all on its own, to think of thwarting old man Everly.

But what really made Trent agree to the deal was his own soft spot for Chase, his childhood friend. He'd agreed to take Chase's place. Minus the saint and celibacy stuff, of course. He was willing to help Susannah by presenting himself *at* the altar, not *on* it.

And look where he'd ended up anyhow. Lying right on that slab. Staring at the longest, coldest year of his life, beside a marble-hearted bitch who just happened to look like a girl he used to love.

But at least Chase was happy. And that was still worth protecting.

Finally resigned, Trent showered and headed back to Everly.

The house had seen better days—it could definitely use a coat of paint—but the fancy gingerbread Victorian looked its best on this cloudless spring morning, with roses bunched up everywhere, and the trees finally back in leaf.

The minute he opened the door, he heard voices. Susannah was here, but she wasn't alone. He listened a second, and recognized Chase.

He scanned the large honey-pine foyer. The guest powder room door was open, the frilly area empty. No sign of Josie. So Chase had come alone.

Had Susannah sent out an SOS? *Needed, one shoulder to cry on, because my husband is a beast.*

"Hey!" Chase stood up from the table as Trent entered the kitchen. He grinned. "You owe me one, buddy. I just barely managed to keep Pastor Wilcox from coming over here. I told him I'd bring his present along, since I was going to stop by anyhow."

Trent was surprised to discover how much the sight of Chase's easy smile annoyed him—especially since he'd just been waxing sentimental about honoring the bond of friendship, taking one for your mate, all that band of brothers nonsense.

But he'd just gotten married last night, for God's sake. Shouldn't your band of brothers be willing to back off for at least one day? Give you time to…

Time to what? To break promises and fling insults? To call each other names and rip open old wounds? Maybe, when he thought about it, he and Susannah had already had all the togetherness they needed.

Trent glanced at her now, standing at the stove. In her usual outfit of sharp khaki slacks and white oxford-cloth shirt, with her hair in a glossy braid down her back, not a strand out of place, she looked utterly serene.

She turned gracefully and held out a blue mug, smiling. "Cup of coffee, Trent? It's fresh."

Her voice was angelic, smooth, as if she'd just this minute set aside her golden harp and stepped down from her cloud. He hesitated a beat before accepting the coffee, sorting the clues.

One thing was clear. She hadn't invited Chase over. She was improvising, pretending that there was smooth sailing in the newlywed world. They weren't going to tell Chase about last night's nosedive into the emotional swamp.

"Okay, thanks," Trent said, playing along. He turned to Chase. "Yeah, we owe you."

But he wasn't sure what to say next. Chase knew them both so well. He wasn't going to be easily fooled.

Trent took a sip of coffee, though it was technically still too hot. Then he reached across the table for the present, wrapped in its flocked silver paper, and picked it up.

"So what did Pastor Wilcox send? I hope it's not one of his wife's samplers. I'll never forget the one in her living room that said 'Enquire not what boils in another's pot.' I swear the thing gave me nightmares."

Chase and Susannah both laughed politely, which in itself was stilted, since this was an old joke. The three of them had made fun of that sampler for years, rewriting it into a hundred vulgar variations, like "Enquire not what rots in another's boils."

He pulled off the white bow and began to rip away the paper, just as if he gave a damn what was inside. They watched him, pretending to be equally transfixed.

It was a picture frame, arranged facedown, so that all he could see was the velvet backing and little gold clips. He flipped it over and readied himself to make some joke about Jenny Wilcox's nutty quotations.

The joke died on his lips. It wasn't a sampler, after all. It was a photograph of Susannah and Trent, standing out in one of the Everly peach orchards. It must have been taken a long time ago. At least eleven years, in fact, because Susannah was laughing, something she hadn't done in Trent's presence since the night of the fire.

She wore a flower-sprigged gypsy dress, and her

skirt was full of peaches. She held the fabric up in both hands, just high enough to expose her knees.

Trent was staring at her, goofy and love-struck, peaches littered around his feet. He had been juggling them, and when Susannah lifted her dress, they'd all come tumbling down.

For an aching instant, just looking at the picture, he was there again, at the church picnic, with Pastor Wilcox taking snapshots. Trent could feel the summer sun on his cheeks, and he could taste the sweet, sticky peaches on his tongue. He had made love to Susannah that night, lying under the moonlight on the cooling grass, and she had tasted of peaches, too.

He glanced up at her now, to see how she had reacted. The past had been so alive that it shocked him to see how different the real Susannah was. Not much older, amazingly, and not any less beautiful, but somehow muffled. Empty, as if whatever spring had fed the laughter had dried up and turned to dust.

Though she, too, stared at the picture, she hadn't reacted at all. She still wore that lovely robot smile. The eyes above it were as empty as a doll's.

He held the picture out. It was cruel, perhaps, but he wanted her to touch it. He wanted her to say something, anything, that proved she was still a real human being.

She took it in her hand. "What a lovely thought," she said blandly, looking down at it without blinking. "That was nice of them."

Then she set it on the table gently. "I'm sorry to leave you, boys, but I've got to talk to the foreman about some new hires. Several of my best workers had a terrible car accident last weekend, and I'm going to be shorthanded."

Obediently, Chase stood up and kissed her on the cheek. She smiled, and waited for Trent to do the same. Still part of the charade for Chase's benefit. Trent kissed her, surprised to find that her cheeks were still soft and warm, not firm plastic like a mannequin's.

Then she was gone.

The silence in the kitchen held a million unasked questions—and a million unspoken answers. Trent didn't rush to fill it. Between the two men, words were often unnecessary.

Chase pulled open the cabinet door that hid the trash can. Then he wadded up the wrapping paper and tossed it toward the container. He missed. Trent retrieved it and tried again. He missed, too.

"Pathetic," Chase said. They both stood staring at the misshapen ball of glittering silver paper on the tiled floor.

"Look, Trent. Maybe I should stay out of this but... don't give up on Sue, okay? It's early days, you know. Things could get better, with a little time."

Trent grunted, then went over and stuffed the paper into the trash can and kicked the cabinet door closed. "Yeah, and you could get drafted by the Mavericks, but I'm not holding my breath."

Chase shook his head. "What the hell happened? I was hoping I'd find you two still in bed. But I get here, you're gone, and she's doing her bookkeeping like it's just any other day. Damn it. I honestly thought that, once you guys were married, she might—"

"Well, she didn't. And she's not going to. I was an idiot to think she ever would. She was always strong, Chase, but it's different now. She's changed. Maybe her grandfather did it to her. Hell, maybe *I* did it. But she's turned…tough."

"No, she hasn't." Chase chewed the inside of his lip. "Or if she is tough, it's tough like an avocado. Just on the outside. You've got to remember that, you know. She can still be bruised on the inside. Are you sure you didn't do something, say something that might have made her feel—"

"No." Trent took his coffee cup to the large stainless steel sink and tossed the dregs down the drain. "I didn't say a damn thing. And, frankly, I'd prefer not to get lectures from you on this. Why don't you go home and take care of your own wife?"

Chase smiled. One of his best traits was his easy nature. He rarely took offense at anything.

"Gladly," he said. "But I think you're passing up some pretty useful advice. After all, I do have an embarrassingly happy marriage."

Trent made a harsh sound. "Then your advice is no use to me. Last night made one thing perfectly clear. Susannah and I aren't *married*." He felt his shoulders tighten. "We're at war."

As Susannah sat with her foreman in his cluttered office just off the barn, listening to him sputter indignantly about the young slacker they'd just interviewed, she really was trying to focus. Every time her mind or her gaze wandered toward the house, she dragged it back.

She had been more relieved to see Trent show up this morning than she wanted to admit. When she'd awakened and found him gone, she hadn't been sure whether he was ever coming back.

But he had come, and that's all that mattered. As long as her plan to break her grandfather's will was safe, she didn't care what Chase and Trent were saying now. Trent had undoubtedly already spilled all the gory details, and they'd begun bashing her, employing the usual macho insults for women who promise things they refuse to deliver.

But so what? That wasn't important. This was. The peach crop was going to be good this year, and, even if she wasn't sure she had buyers for the fruit, she'd still need as many skilled workers as possible to bring it in.

Even the worker she'd just interviewed. Eli Breslin.

"I couldn't believe it when I saw the cheeky little son of a gun." Zander was so outraged he sputtered. "He has the nerve to walk in here? As if you'd hire *that one* to shine your shoes!"

She smiled. "I can't afford to have my shoes shined by *anybody*. But I do need someone to pick peaches. And he's the only one who showed up, right?"

"Well." Zander shuffled papers on his desk. "There were a few calls."

"Yes, but those men weren't good enough, either."

They'd already discussed this. One candidate used to work for the Ritchie spread, which was notoriously badly run, and the second applicant had been on the wagon for only six months, which wasn't long enough in Zander's eyes, and…well, the bottom line seemed to be that most of the callers failed to meet the foreman's standards.

Eli Breslin wouldn't have made the cut, either, except that he hadn't bothered to phone first. He'd just knocked on the office door, and Susannah, despairing of getting anyone past Zander's gauntlet, had insisted on interviewing the kid.

Zander leaned back in his ancient, squeaking leather chair and tapped his pencil against his knee. "He's got zero experience with peaches."

"He can learn," Susannah said. She moved her hand and almost overturned a teetering stack of paperwork. Ironic that Zander required perfection of everyone but himself. "Things are desperate right now. We may have to lower our standards a bit."

Of course, that was the wrong thing to say. The big man sat up straight and puffed out his chest. "I'm glad your grandfather isn't around to hear you say such a thing. He never abandoned his standards, no matter what. Not even when the Alzheimer's laid him low."

Sighing, Susannah stood and walked to the window, where she could see the east forty, which looked beautiful in May, with all the trees wearing full green. The sight calmed her a little.

She and Zander had been through this a dozen times in the two years since Arlington H. Everly had died, and she didn't feel like hashing it out again.

Her grandfather's "standards" were, in her view, simply mule-headed stubbornness and excessive pride. His refusal to face economic facts had brought Everly to this current disaster, and she and Zander both knew it.

When Susannah was a kid, before her parents died, Everly Industries had owned ten thousand acres of fertile land here near Austin, and almost as many in West Texas, where the land was so rich the oil just boiled out of the ground. Today, they had one tenth that, only one thousand acres, a mere three hundred of them producing. Oh, and a dried-up two-acre plot in West Texas that looked like Swiss cheese from all the useless holes Arlington had kept drilling after Alzheimer's had claimed his brain.

"I need hands," she said, trying to stick to the topic. "Lots of hands to prune and thin, and then, in a few weeks, start bringing in those peaches before they rot on the trees. Eli Breslin is a healthy, willing worker with two excellent hands. Hire him."

The silence behind her was full of disapproval. Finally Zander spoke, his voice a deep, censorious rumble in his chest. "You can't mean that. What about Miss Nikki?"

She bit her lower lip. That was the big question, of course. When Eli Breslin had worked next door at Chase's Double C quarter horse ranch, Nikki had fallen for him like a too-ripe peach dropping from the tree. In fact, Eli Breslin was one of the main reasons Susannah had decided to spring for Nikki's expensive art school. It had simply been too hard to keep the two from sneaking off together into the orchard late at night.

And Susannah knew all too well what could happen in the orchard, under a milky moon, on a warm spring night.

On the other hand, Nikki *was* gone, and during his

interview Eli had apologized with a lot of grace and maturity. Maybe, without her wild little sister to distract him, Eli Breslin could be a good worker.

Or maybe Zander was right. Maybe Eli was just too iffy....

She pressed her hand over her eyes. She'd been staring out into the sun too long, and she was getting a headache.

She heard someone open the office door behind her, and then the sound of Zander levering himself out of his squeaky chair.

"Trent! Thank God you're here! Maybe you can help me talk some sense into Ms. Susannah!"

Oh, great. She needed this right now.

Susannah turned to see Trent moving into the office, his lean height dominating it more thoroughly than even Zander's bulk could ever do. He shut the door behind him, then came over and shook the foreman's outstretched hand, simultaneously slapping him on the shoulder. They were old friends, and suddenly she felt outnumbered.

"No one needs to talk sense into me." She included both men in her scowl. But damn it. What was it about Trent's lazy, amused grin that made her feel like a kid stamping her foot? "I make my own decisions. I know what I'm doing."

Trent raised his eyebrow, as if she'd said something cute, and transferred that annoying grin to the foreman. "Come on, Zan. You know her. When she makes a decision, you and I and Hell's army couldn't talk her out of it. Save your energy for a battle you can win."

"I would. God knows, I usually do. But this is different. She's getting ready to hire Eli Breslin."

Trent's eyebrow went up even farther. "Really?" He glanced at Susannah. "Why?"

"Because I need workers, that's why. Because Eli applied, and he sounded sincere about needing the job. He went out of his way to apologize for everything that happened with Nikki. He explained that he was just lonesome. Homesick. That's why he wants a second job now, to save up to buy a plane ticket back home to El Cajon."

Trent chuckled. "He actually said that?"

"You should have heard the little weasel." Zander grimaced. "Kid should be an actor. He spread honey on her like she was his own personal biscuit. Ninety-three percent of it pure baloney, if you ask me."

"But I didn't." Susannah tightened her voice. "I didn't ask either of you. It's my decision."

Zander growled under his breath, like a fussy old hound. "You do remember what he did at the Clayton place, don't you? You remember he walked away from a sick horse, didn't care whether the animal lived or died? You remember Trent had to fire him?"

"She remembers." Trent's smile was gone. In its place was cool speculation. "Is that part of the appeal, Susannah? Do you think it would be fun to tweak my nose a bit?"

It might be *fun,* she thought, to see if she could slap that insufferable arrogance off his face. But she gritted her teeth and braided her hands behind her back. Her famous self-control was the only thing that kept Zander from quitting. She'd heard him say it was beneath him to work for a woman, but Ms. Everly didn't really act like one, so he didn't mind too much.

She lifted her chin. "As I've pointed out before, Trent, not everything I do is about you."

But he just grinned again, and her palms itched. How did he do this to her? Why couldn't she learn to be immune to his snarky comments and his laughing eyes?

She had been vacillating about Eli, but suddenly her mind was made up.

She moved to the door, opened it, then turned to her foreman. "Hire him. Ask him if he has a brother, an uncle, a dog. Hire them all."

"Dumb decision," Zander muttered. "You'll regret it."

"Oh, I wouldn't worry about that," Trent said pleasantly. Susannah had let the door begin to fall shut, so she almost missed the rest of the comment.

But his words were loud enough to follow her, like a dart finding its bull's eye.

"Our Susannah's a clever woman, Zan. Trust me. If she regrets it, she can always find a way to wriggle out of it."

CHAPTER THREE

AT THREE O'CLOCK that afternoon, Trent knocked at the baby blue door of a little white cottage over in Darlonsville.

"Trent!" Peggy Archer held out her hand. Her eyes were wide, and she seemed momentarily speechless. "I didn't expect to see you today. Shouldn't you be with… her?"

Trent sensed the trembling in her fingers and squeezed them reassuringly. "I've had a date with you every Saturday afternoon for five years now, Peggy. Marriage isn't going to change that."

She nodded slowly. "Especially *that* marriage."

"Not *any* marriage. You told me your satellite dish is broken. I know you can't live without your Sunday night football."

He smiled, aware that Peggy never watched sports on TV, but hoping to distract her from the subject of Susannah. It was a sore one in this house.

Long ago, when they were kids, Peggy's son Paul had been part of the inseparable quartet, the Fugitive Four. Trent, Chase and Susannah had all been Peggy's surrogate children, eating her corn dogs and hot chili every summer afternoon at the Bull's Eye ranch, the ten-thousand-acre Archer homestead.

But then, eleven years ago, a quarrel between Trent and Susannah had escalated into tragedy, and Peggy's son, Paul, had ended up dead. It had been about ninety-nine percent Trent's fault, and it had taken him years to find the courage to come back to Texas and face what he'd done.

Facing Peggy had been the toughest. But little by little, she had forgiven him and let him slip into the role of surrogate son once more. Oddly, as the years had gone on, she had ended up blaming Susannah the most.

When Trent had told her about the one-year marriage, the news had seemed to distress her out of all proportion. Trent had assumed it had been because of Paul, but he wondered now if Peggy had simply feared she'd lose Trent's weekly visit.

Darn it. Foolishly, he'd taken for granted that she would understand. He'd never stop coming to see her, not as long as she needed him.

His debt to her was eternal. It would never be paid.

He tightened his grip on her hand. "Hey. Don't I get invited in?"

"Of course, but—" She glanced over her shoulder as she backed away from the door. "I thought you weren't coming, so—"

Just at that moment, her ex-husband, Harrison Archer, ambled in from the kitchen, muttering under his breath and studying the bracket that ordinarily held the satellite dish up on the roof.

Harrison was a balding, Texas-sized good old boy with a chest as round and barrel-shaped as any of his steers. At his heels trailed his son Sean, who at eight years old already looked shockingly like Paul. Both sons from Harrison's second marriage did. It was the red hair, mostly. Harrison's new wife, Nora, was half Peggy's age, but otherwise could have been her clone—same fiery hair, petite body and smart hazel eyes.

Everyone knew what Harrison was doing when he married Nora, only two years after Paul's death. He was doubling back to square one and starting over. Or trying to. But in spite of the healthy new sons and the pretty wife, there was still something dead in his eyes that made Trent uncomfortable whenever their gazes met.

"Trent. Thank God you're here." Harrison held up the bracket. "I can't figure this blame thing out to save my life. And Sean has a game tonight. All right if I let you take over?"

"Sure." Trent smiled at Harrison and then at Sean, who was a cute kid, gangly in his miniature polyester Red Sox uniform. "Hi, kiddo."

"Sean is pitching today," Harrison said in his deepest proud-father voice, his chest expanding subtly, stretching the buttons of his five-hundred-dollar denim shirt.

Trent wasn't sure how to respond. For starters, he couldn't believe the man had brought Sean here suited up like this, like the ghost of Paul. Mentioning the pitching was almost unbelievably insensitive.

But the kid looked excited, so Trent couldn't just ignore it. "Oh, yeah? Cool."

Sean grinned. "I'm working on my knuckleball. Dad says I'm getting pretty good."

Instinctively, Trent shot a glance at Peggy. Once, Paul had pitched for the high school team. He'd been good—almost great. A&M had offered him a full scholarship. But at the very moment when he should have been reporting for practice, he'd been lying in a hospital bed.

Burned over seventy percent of his body.

Dying.

And now Harrison was teaching the famous Archer knuckleball to this freckle-faced replacement son. Peggy stared at the wall, apparently determined not to look at Sean. Her cheeks were pale, her hazel eyes ominously glassy. Trent's shoulders tightened. It was like torture, rubbing salt in a wound that already refused to heal.

"I need to sit down." Peggy let go of Trent's hand and led the way into the small blue-and-white living room.

Her limp was worse this week, Trent noticed. She must be in a lot of pain. Though only in her early fifties, she moved like a woman of ninety. Her hip replacement surgery was scheduled for July, a long six weeks from now. She was dreading it, but Trent privately hoped it would give her a sort of fresh start, too.

Harrison set the bracket down on the coffee table, not bothering to hide his eagerness to escape. "So, you can handle this alone, right? It's not that big a job, and we probably should hit the road. Nora gets out of Pilates at four, and she needs to shower before the game."

"Yeah, I'll be fine." Trent repressed the urge to shake the older man. Was he doing this deliberately? Why would he mention Nora's daily exercise class, when his ex-wife could barely walk?

As if Peggy didn't already know that a heartbroken, postmenopausal arthritic could never hold a candle to the buoyant young wife who waited for Harrison at home.

"Good. Well, then, we'll be going." Harrison looked over at Peggy, who had lowered herself into a white rocker and picked up her knitting, as if to say, *Yes, I'm a middle-aged woman, and I don't care.* "Goodbye, then, Peg."

"Bye, Peggy," Sean echoed politely. "Thanks for having me."

She didn't look up from her yarn. "Goodbye."

The word was so cold it sent a small gust of frigid air out into the room. Bristling, Harrison drew his eyebrows together. He handed his son the car keys and whispered something. Sean nodded and headed toward the front stairs.

As soon as the door shut behind the boy, Harrison turned and glared at his ex-wife. "None of this is Sean's fault, you know," he said gruffly.

She kept knitting. Her fingers looked almost as white as the yarn.

"Damn it, Peggy. You could be a little nicer to him."

She finally looked up. "No. As a matter of fact, Harry, I couldn't. Don't ever bring that boy into my house again."

Harrison made a sharp move forward, but Trent threw out his arm. He'd seen the Archer temper all too often in the old days. Back then, he'd been too young, too intimidated by the Archer acres, to know what he should do about it.

But he knew now.

"Hey," he said. *"Easy."*

The older man's chest pushed against Trent's forearm, as if he might put up a fight. His breath came harsh and heavy. They stood that way about ten seconds, with Harrison clearly struggling for composure.

Finally he eased back an inch or two. He transferred his glare to Trent. "I need to talk to you, son," he said. "Outside."

Trent didn't much like the autocratic tone, but he very much liked the idea of getting the agitated man away from Peggy. He nodded and followed Harrison through the door and onto the front porch.

"Bitch," Harrison muttered as the door shut behind him. Trent ignored it, but he placed himself between the older man and the entry, just in case.

"You said you wanted to talk to me?"

Harrison took one last deep breath, and ran his hands through his thinning brown hair. "Look, I'm sorry. I shouldn't have lost my temper. It's just that even after all these years, she can still get my goat. She's stuck in the past, Trent. Damn it, I loved Paul, too, but I have to get on with my life, don't I? And she hates me for it."

"Maybe she just hates having your new life thrown in her face."

Harrison's fleshy cheeks reddened. "Thrown in her face? Look, I didn't choose to come here. *She* called *me.* She said she needed help. And look what it turned out to be! The damn television set!"

Trent didn't bother to try to make Harrison understand how important television could be to someone as lonely as Peggy. Empathy wasn't the man's strong suit.

"Well, I'm here now, so you're off the hook. Take Sean to the game and forget about it."

"It's ridiculous, anyhow." Harrison glanced toward the house with distaste. "Why the hell didn't she just hire someone to fix it? God knows the allowance I give her is big enough."

Trent's jaw was so tight he could hardly get words out. "I think she likes the company. Half the time when I come over, she tells me to forget the repairs. She just wants to sit and talk."

Harrison laughed. "What? You think she just likes to hang out with you? Don't kid yourself, son. She's using you. She knows you've got a guilty conscience, so she plays on it."

Trent had heard enough. "You know, I think it's time for you to go."

To his surprise, the edict didn't seem to inflame the older man's tinderbox temper. Instead, Harrison's face softened, as if swept by a sudden and rare compassion. "You really care about her, don't you?"

"Yes."

"Poor kid." Harrison rested his meaty hand gently on Trent's shoulder. "I know you think you can make it up to her. But you can't. It's too big, what happened."

Trent shrugged. "Maybe. I come because I like to. That's all."

"Okay." Harrison nodded, but he chewed on the inside of his cheek as if something troubled him. "Still…you need to watch your step, son. Because I promise you this. Deep down inside where nobody sees, that woman *hates* you."

THOUGH MONDAY was only Eli Breslin's first day, by midafternoon Susannah was guardedly pleased with his performance. During the lunch break, when Zander and Susannah had gone over business in the foreman's office, even the older man had grudgingly admitted that, *so far,* the boy took instruction meekly and worked hard.

Maybe too hard. Mid-May in Central Texas could be cool, but summer was sneaking in early this year, and temperatures were already hitting eighty.

When Susannah drove the flatbed out to see how the tree thinning was coming along, she caught a glimpse of Eli, leaning against the bright yellow shaking machine, dirty and sweaty and shirtless. He held a plastic water bottle above his head and was letting its contents pour over his upturned face and run glistening down his sunburned chest.

For the first time, Susannah could sort of see why Nikki had fallen for him. He did have that hunky blond surfer boy thing going on big-time.

And that had always been Nikki's type.

Susannah, on the other hand, had always been fatally drawn to the black-haired, blue-eyed dangerous devil thing. So when this sweaty young sexpot smiled wetly over at her, the only thing she felt was mild anxiety. He was so fair-skinned…would that mean he was susceptible to heatstroke?

A sudden pang pierced just under her ribs. She wished that things could have been different. If only she and Nikki could have been normal sisters. If only they could have laughed about boys, shared secrets, conspired to hide mischief from their parents. Instead, because their mother and father had died when Susannah was fifteen, and Nikki only a toddler, Susannah had been forced into the role of surrogate mother.

How Nikki had hated it, all these years. She had no idea that Susannah had hated it, too. But she did—she hated the injustice of it. They'd both been cheated of their parents. But they'd also been cheated of each other. Even after Nikki passed through adolescence, they would probably never have the tight friendship that real sisters should have.

Susannah squeezed her eyes, as if she could squeeze away the self-pity. She didn't have time to lament tragedies that had happened so long ago. She couldn't change the past. All she could hope was that maybe she could keep the present and future from capsizing, too.

Suddenly, Zander was at Susannah's elbow, wiping a dirty rag across his own sweaty face. "Little brat broke the shaking machine."

"What?"

Susannah looked again toward Eli and realized belatedly that the machine should not have been silent and still. It should have been roaring and grumbling away, moving among the trees, grabbing trunks with its tail-like pincers, and jostling dime-sized peaches from branches like a blush-colored rain.

She sniffed, and finally she smelled it—the stench of steam and burning rubber wafting through the orchard, a dark undercurrent below the sweetness of the fruit-littered ground.

Eli seemed to think she was staring at him, because he smiled again, carving dimples into his cheeks. He pointed the empty water bottle toward the shaking machine, then used it to draw an imaginary line across his throat.

The message was clear. The machine was dead. And Eli thought it was mildly amusing.

Well, he could afford to consider this a little gift from the go-home-early gods, but Susannah wanted to cuss. It could take days to get it repaired. And now that every fruit grower in central Texas was in the throes of thinning season, where would she be able to borrow another one in the meantime?

"I knew it was too good to be true," Zander muttered. "I knew all this perfect employee crap was just an act."

"It's not Eli's fault." Somehow Susannah kept her voice cool. "It broke on you last year, too, Zander. It's just old. We need a new one."

"We can't afford a new one."

She slapped her work gloves into the palm of her hand, trying to hold back the retort that sprang to her lips. Of course she knew they couldn't afford one. If they hadn't been in dire straits, did Zander think she would have sold herself into a year of matrimonial bondage?

"Maybe," she said, "Chase will loan us his."

"Yes. You should ask Trent about it ASAP." Zander frowned. "Where is he, anyhow? Haven't seen him around all weekend."

That was, of course, the sixty-four-thousand-dollar question. Where *was* her brand-new husband? He had slept at Everly every night, she knew that. That first night he'd used the sofa, but after that he'd confiscated her grandfather's bedroom. He came in late, then left again early in the morning.

Which was fine with her, of course. The less she saw of him, the better. Still, she couldn't help wondering where he went. To Chase's ranch? Maybe. Running a ranch that large could easily eat up your weekends, too.

But she couldn't help wondering whether he might be going somewhere…softer.

To some*one* softer.

After all, he'd done it before.

She forced the image out of her mind. As long as he satisfied the will's requirements by spending the nights under her roof, she didn't give a damn about his days. And if she kept letting him disrupt her concentration, she was going to be in even bigger trouble than she was already.

Her gaze drifted to the other workers, who were still moving toward them, following the machine's path, hand-thinning the small branches that hadn't let go of their bounty.

So much to do…so many people to pay.

Her mind began performing calculations at warp speed. If this was a big repair, and it sure smelled that way, it would eat into the payroll, and then she'd be behind on the—

"Die, you bastard! Die!"

Her heart pounding, she wheeled quickly, just in time to see that Eli had grabbed a shovel and was violently slashing at the ground, just a couple of yards away from the shaker's cab.

For a split second, as he jumped and hollered, she wondered whether Zander and Trent been right about Eli all along. Had she hired a madman?

But then she saw the rubbery-looking, writhing coils at Eli's feet. A shiver sped down her spine.

He was killing a very large rattlesnake.

Though it seemed to be happening in slow motion, it probably was over in less than ten seconds, and the poor creature lay mangled in the dirt, thoroughly destroyed. Several other workers, including Zander, gathered to get a better look.

Eli's cocky smile was gone, and his cheeks were pale beneath the sunburn. He stared down at his palms, bloodied by the pitted metal on the old shovel's handle.

Then he raised a stricken face and glanced over at Susannah, as if he feared he might have done the wrong thing.

"I'm sorry," he said, in a voice that belonged to a much younger boy. "I just saw him there, and I panicked."

If she hadn't been his employer, she would have put her arm around his shoulder, the same way she might have comforted Nikki after a bad day at school. She settled for offering a reassuring smile.

"You did great. Come on, let's go back and get that blood cleaned up. Zander will take care of all this."

She ignored the older man's look of irritation. The boy's hands needed tending. Besides, it was her fault he was hurt. That shovel should have been replaced years ago, like so many other things on this spread.

She sighed as she started the truck, hearing the hesitation of a battery about to go dead.

How many problems could she handle at once?

Five years ago, when Trent had accepted Chase's offer to be the ranch manager at the Double C, he had worked twenty-hour days for more than a year, sleeping on a cot in the office, determined not to let Chase down.

He'd had so much to prove. He knew what everyone had thought when he'd left town six years earlier, after the fire, while Paul still lay dying in that hospital bed.

They'd thought he was a bad-tempered son of a bitch, who had been playing out of his league for years and finally got exposed as the loser he really was. He knew that's what they'd thought, because that was what *he'd* thought, too.

So he'd run. He hadn't known what else to do. The whole tragedy had been too much to stand. He was only nineteen, and he'd messed up everything he cared about in the whole stinking world. He'd cheated on Susannah, and then, in a fit of pique, he'd punched his best friend, and somehow rained disaster down on them all.

Sometimes, now, he could hardly remember how it happened. But sometimes it played over in his head, as if it were a videotape caught in a slow-motion loop.

He had been in a rotten mood that night, furious with himself for succumbing to Missy Snowdon's cheap charms, and praying Susannah would never find out. They'd all gone to a bar for dinner, and he had unwisely let himself drink too much. Susannah and Paul had been flirting, and by the third beer, courtesy of friends older than the legal limit, Trent hadn't been able to pretend he didn't care.

He'd said some things, and Paul had said some things, and before he knew what was happening, his fist had been flying. That was when the nightmare took over. He'd expected Paul to punch him back. He even wanted him to. Somehow he felt that a little pain might make him feel less guilty for what he'd done with Missy.

Instead, Paul tilted back, his jaw hanging open. He waved his arms, trying to catch his balance, but he was already falling, falling, slamming into the bar's picnic table seats, his arms still windmilling like a cartoon.

When he hit the ground, so did the kerosene lantern that had looked so kitschy and cute on the table.

The hay on the floor went up like a magician's trick. Paul caught fire, too, rolling at first, trying to get to his feet, then toppling over like a fireplace log. Trent still heard him scream sometimes, and not just in his dreams. The echo of Paul's pain could come out of nowhere, using the voice of everyday things. The cry of owls, the squeal of children playing. A rusty hinge on an old screen door, or the screech of tires on a dangerous road.

The doctors had tried. Paul clung to life for months, mostly because his parents wouldn't disconnect the machines that kept him breathing. But everyone knew he was gone.

And everyone knew who had killed him. Trent might as well have put a gun to Paul's head and pulled the trigger. In fact, it would have been a more merciful death.

So, as soon as he realized it was hopeless, he'd run as far and as long as his college savings would take him. He'd run until he'd hit the Pacific Ocean, chased by the memories of Paul's mutilated body and the curse in Susannah's cold eyes.

He'd run into another woman's arms, and then another's, and then another's. He'd even married one of them, though thank God she was a smart, cheerful woman, who came to her senses before too long.

When Ginny realized her new husband was little more than a cardboard cutout, a shell of a man, she divorced him as cheerfully as she'd married him.

On his twenty-fifth birthday, he had decided to come home. To face all the ghosts, both the living and the dead. To make amends and, maybe, finally, make something of himself.

But that was five years ago, and he was through proving things. Maybe he could never completely silence Paul's screams, but he had finally learned his own worth. Anyone else who was still unconvinced could just remain that way.

Which was why, when he found himself yawning at work and realized he'd put in about forty hours at this desk in the past two days, he decided that enough was enough.

He was going home. He didn't care whether Susannah was hanging around or not. He was too damn tired to get all hot and bothered, not even if she was dancing on the kitchen table wearing a whipped-cream G-string.

He almost made it back to Everly without getting snagged by work—it was the next spread over, no more than fifteen minutes away—but at the last minute his phone buzzed with a text message from Zander, something about a broken shaker. He was tempted to ignore it, but the old guy sounded stressed, so he made some calls.

By the time he rolled into the Everly drive, he had Chase's extra machine lined up for the next two weeks. Still yawning, he walked to the stables, one end of which had been converted into the foreman's office, to tell Zander the good news.

But Zander wasn't there. Instead, Trent opened the door onto a cozy domestic scene, with Susannah and Eli Breslin sitting knee to knee on Zander's guest chairs. The kid was half-naked and sweaty. Susannah was holding his hand.

Trent frowned, but then it made sense. The moron had managed to get hurt on his very first day.

Susannah was bent over Eli's outstretched fingers, utterly focused on wrapping a bandage around his palm, and her braid fell over her shoulder. She had no idea that Trent had arrived.

But Eli did.

He gave Trent a small smile, which spread across his dirty face until it was a downright nasty grin. Everything Eli had probably heard from gossips about Susannah's new marriage was written in that leer. Trent might have been able to fire Eli from the Double C, but Eli clearly knew that the "husband of convenience" had no power at Everly. He knew that Trent was as much a temporary employee here as Eli himself.

And he wanted Trent to know that he knew.

"Ouch," Eli moaned softly as Susannah worked on the bandage. She murmured an apology for hurting him. The boy smirked down at her, then turned to Trent and slowly winked.

Obnoxious little bastard…

"There. That should hold." Susannah held Eli's hand up for him to inspect. "It looked worse than it was."

Eli bent in close, so that his face was only inches from Susannah's. "Thank you, Ms. Everly. You have mighty gentle hands."

Clearing his throat, Trent moved into the small office, dodging a trophy that teetered on a bookcase, proclaiming Alexander Hobbin to be the 1978 Men's Bowling Champ. If it had fallen over and beaned Eli on the head, that would have been fine with Trent.

"So," he said. "You think your new hire will live to work another day?"

Susannah looked up. If she felt any embarrassment at being caught holding hands with a bare-chested teenage peach picker, she covered it well.

"Yes," she said as she began to store her first aid supplies neatly away. "It was just a little mishap. Minor abrasions."

"I killed a rattler," Eli put in, stretching out his legs and leaning back in his chair nonchalantly, as if he performed such feats every day. "Nasty, big one. Five feet, at least."

"Taller than you are, then?" Trent smiled. "Impressive."

"No." Eli flushed angrily. "I'm five ten and a half."

"And a *half!*" Trent raised his eyebrow. "Also impressive. I wouldn't have guessed."

The boy's face was a thundercloud. "Yeah, well, I hear that you—"

"Trent." Susannah snapped the first aid kit shut and gave Trent a look that said *enough already.*

She was right, of course. It was ridiculous to get into an ego-tussle with a nineteen-year-old. But apparently, where Susannah was concerned, a part of Trent would always be nineteen. Ready to lock horns with any other young buck who tried to trespass on his turf.

"Did you need something, Trent? Were you looking for Zander? He's still out in the orchard, finishing up the thinning."

"He messaged me about the shaker. I wanted to let him know we've rearranged things at the Double C so that you can use Chase's machine for the next couple of weeks."

"You don't need to borrow one," Eli broke in eagerly, like the smarmy teacher's pet everyone had hated in high school. "I'm good with machines. I bet I could fix ours."

Ours? The kid had worked here one half of one day, and already he owned the equipment? Trent turned toward the brat, ready to let loose, but Susannah put out her hand and touched Trent's forearm lightly.

"Thanks, Eli," she said, "but unless you can actually raise the dead, I'm afraid it's no use. We'll be fine with the loaner. Please go let Mr. Hobbin know it's arranged, okay?"

Eli was caught for a moment, wedged between his desire to avenge himself with Trent and his determination to impress Susannah.

Self-preservation won the day. He bobbed his head deferentially. "Yes, ma'am. Thank you, ma'am."

After he was gone, the silence in the office was fraught with tension.

Susannah put the kit away, locked the cabinet and

then finally turned to Trent. "Please tell Chase thanks. I appreciate the loan of the shaker."

For some inexplicable reason, Trent was suddenly irritated. For one thing, Chase didn't even know about the loan. Trent was in charge of all such details at the Double C. It was Trent who had made it possible.

But clearly there'd be snowball fights in Hell before Susannah would ever thank Trent for anything.

She lifted her chin. "Was there anything else you needed?"

That ice-cold tone was the last straw. "Yeah," he said. "One other thing. I thought I'd just mention what a colossally bad idea it is to flirt with teenage boys who happen to be on your payroll."

Her eyebrows dived together. "I wasn't *flirting* with him."

"Really? Are you sure he knows that?"

"I'm quite sure." She stood ramrod straight, clearly offended. "Is that why you were being such an ass to him? Because you thought we were…flirting?"

Trent sat on the corner of Zander's desk, the only spot not covered in files and papers and junk. "No, I was being an ass to him because he is a cocky little loser who hasn't ever done an honest day's work in his life, and I can't believe you were dumb enough to hire him."

She'd gone slightly pale, which he knew from long experience was a sign of fury. He braced himself for the storm, and as he did he realized that, in some strange way, he welcomed the fight.

At least it would be real emotion. A real connection.

And, God help him, he still craved that. All that crap about being too exhausted to desire her? He'd been sunk the minute he saw the curve of her back as she'd bent over Eli's hand, and the way the sunlight created a halo around her head.

It had been enough to send the hunger raging through him all over again. He wouldn't get what he really wanted, of course. But a good, rousing battle might at least siphon off some of this tension.

She took a couple of deep breaths, obviously determined to hold on to her temper. She placed herself behind the desk, as if she thought its scarred oak surface could provide the buffer zone she clearly needed.

But it wasn't a very big desk.

"How I run Everly is none of your business." She straightened some papers on the desk, a ridiculously futile gesture. "That wasn't part of our deal."

Her fingers trembled as they nudged another sheet of paper into line. The pause stretched until it shimmered in the room like ectoplasm.

"Oh, yes," he said slowly. "The *deal*."

She didn't look up. But her grip tightened, crumpling the edge of the file she held.

"The deal," he repeated. He reached out and took her wrist between his fingers. "We did have one, didn't we?"

She tensed, though she didn't try to pull back her hand. "Trent, I don't think we should—"

"I do."

She lifted her chin. "Look, I know you're angry."

He ran his thumb across the inside of her wrist, until

he found the pulse, jumping and skittering between the delicate bones. "Am I?"

"Well, you've been gone all weekend. I'm not a fool, Trent. I know what that means."

He thought of Peggy, of the secret trips he'd been making to Darlonsville for five years now. He hadn't wanted anyone to know. He hadn't wanted to look as if he did it only for the good public relations it might bring.

"And what do you think it means?"

"It means…" She bit her lower lip. "I know where you must have been, who you must have been with. Even though, when we agreed to do this, you promised me that there would be no other women, not while we were married."

He tugged her wrist slightly. She either had to wrestle herself free or come around the desk to meet him. She chose to come around, though it brought her close enough that he could see the nervous twitch next to the corner of her mouth.

Ah…she felt more fear now than anger. In a perverse way, that pleased him. It proved he still had power.

And he saw something else, too. A physical awareness of him that heated the surface of her cheeks.

It made him ache, being so close to her, smelling her, hating her and wanting her all at the same time. It was as if someone had shoved a hot brand against the small of his back.

"I did promise I'd be faithful," he said, careful to keep his tone lightly ironic. "But that was when I believed I'd be getting what I needed here at home…within the marriage bed, so to speak."

"Yes," she said quickly. "Yes, of course I see the difference. So that's why I wanted to make you an offer. I understand that it's a…a hardship to have to…to do without sex for a full year, and…"

He smiled. Her pulse had tripped on itself from the effort to even say the word *sex*.

"And?"

She swallowed, blinking as she tried to hold his gaze. "And I'd like to make it up to you. Financially, I mean. I was thinking ten thousand dollars for every month we're married. That's one hundred and twenty thousand dollars, when the year is up, when I can sell the acres I need, and—"

He tilted his head, chuckling softly. "You're offering to pay me not to have sex with you?"

"No…I'm paying you for not having it with anyone else, not while we're married. It's hard to—" She swallowed and tried again. "If you have a mistress while I'm your wife, it'll be—well, everyone will say it's just like before. I'll be the laughing stock of Texas. I'd prefer not to be shamed like that…not again."

He cursed inwardly. It always came back to that, didn't it? Eleven years ago, he'd made a mistake, and, in her eyes, it would forever define the man he was. He felt his hand tighten on her wrist, as the frustration, the anger and the hunger tied every muscle in his body into knots.

"You must agree it's generous, Trent. A hundred and twenty thousand—"

"Oh, sure. It's generous."

He couldn't stand it anymore. Without thinking, he

pulled her toward him. She wasn't expecting it, and she stumbled, practically falling into his arms. Her body was stiff, but her flesh trembled. He let his palms encircle her waist, and they met around the slim curves, just as they used to do.

She stared up at him. He didn't apologize, didn't let go. He stroked her rib cage with his thumbs.

"Trent..."

"Your offer is generous as hell, Susannah. But money isn't what I want." He angled her even closer, close enough to feel the heat that throbbed through him. "You know what I want."

"But what you want—you can't...what about the paper?" She seemed to be struggling to catch a breath, inhaling softly between each word. "You won't...sign it?"

"No, I won't sign it, Sue, but there are other ways."

"Other ways to...what?"

Her lips were half-open, peach-pink wet and glimmering in the sunlight. They were ripe and soft. And he remembered exactly how they had tasted. How they had felt, on him, around him. For eleven long years, even in dreams, he had been haunted by the memory of their warmth, their hidden strength....

A painful heat swelled inside him. She might hate him, but he must have this. He refused to go on burning and wanting, and being forever denied.

Though she wouldn't admit it, she burned, too, and he would follow that fiery path until he found his way in.

"Trent. Tell me what you mean."

He let his body answer her. He placed his palms against her buttocks, and moved her hips toward him slowly, by agonizing inches, letting his heat find hers. He watched what it did to her. He watched her eyes struggle not to lose focus, watched her throat hold back the moan that wanted to break free.

Somehow she hung on to her question, as if it were a life raft, as if it could take her to a different answer. "Other ways for what?"

"Other ways for husbands and wives to know each other. Please each other. Ways that don't risk making babies."

She stopped breathing entirely. "You can't mean—"

"Yes, I can. There are lots of ways to make love, Susannah." Trent let her go abruptly, smiled and moved toward the door. "And before this year is over, we're going to discover every one of them."

CHAPTER FOUR

IT WASN'T EASY to sleep that night. Every noise Susannah heard, even the familiar oak branch that had scratched against her window since she was six, made her heart race. Outside, the night seemed to go on forever, the mushroom-colored moon caught in a soup of gray clouds. Inside, every creaking floorboard, every snap, groan or sigh from the old house, sounded like Trent coming to find her.

Trent, coming to lie beside her in the darkness and, with his angry lips and determined hands, somehow force her to keep her promise.

She woke up feeling wrung out and muddy-headed. And oddly lonely. In some ways, she missed Nikki. It would have been nice to have someone to talk to. But sitting around gabbing was a luxury she could rarely afford—and it wasn't something Nikki enjoyed much, anyhow. So she tried just to be glad she didn't have to make breakfast for Nikki and nag her out the door to school.

She did have to get up, though. She was due at the burn center by nine, and there was no way to avoid it. She went in only two mornings a week during peach season, and Rachel, her gung-ho administrative assistant, would undoubtedly have scheduled a dozen meetings, phone calls and interviews.

So Susannah put on her best spring suit and extra lipstick, and made her way across town. She sent up a little prayer that no big problems would present themselves today, and that maybe she could get home early.

No such luck.

"Susannah, thank God you're here." Rachel stood up from her chair when she saw her boss. "You're not going to believe what Dr. Mahaffey's wife did."

Susannah moved into her office and put down her purse, trying to refrain from pointing out that she didn't care what Dr. Mahaffey's wife did. Obviously, she couldn't say such a thing. Dr. Mahaffey was the retired chief of surgery for the burn center, and his wife had organized some of their most successful fund-raisers. So what Mrs. Mahaffey did was always important.

Especially to the executive coordinator of donor/volunteer affairs. And that was Susannah.

"What did she do?" Susannah managed a smile, because she knew the answer would be something hilarious. Spunky, opinionated, energetic Maggie Mahaffey was eighty-two, nine years older than her exhausted husband, and most of the time she lived on Mars.

Rachel stood in the doorway between the offices and held out a plate heaped with pie. "She sent in a recipe for the peach book."

Susannah set down the stack of color-coded phone messages she'd just grabbed and stared at the plate, as if she expected it to explode. "Oh, no."

"Oh, yes." Rachel nodded, her full lips pressed so tightly you almost couldn't see her signature-red lipstick. "Taste it."

Susannah laughed and took a step backward. "I'll take your word for it. What's wrong this time? Six pounds of sugar? How that woman has managed to avoid diabetes is a mystery to me."

"No sugar. This time she added mint." Rachel widened her eyes dramatically. "*Mint.* And...*cashews.*"

Susannah's mouth just hung open, seemingly unable to respond to her order to close. "Cashews in her peach pie?"

"Yes. *Cashews.*" Rachel wasn't easily rattled, but this clearly had shaken her. "What are we going to do, Susannah? It's indescribably gross. I brushed my teeth twice, and I still taste it."

Susannah sat on the edge of her desk, suddenly tired. Given what she was going through back at Everly, a disgusting peach pie simply didn't seem important. "I'll just have to create a typo. The line about the cashews will mysteriously drop off."

"Again? You did that last year, with the sugar! Mrs. Mahaffey tried to get you fired then. If you do it again, she'll have your head."

"She's welcome to it." Susannah reached one more time for the phone messages. Red meant "urgent" and the stack was about ninety percent red. "Did the volunteer training session go all right?"

Rachel set the pie down on her desk, giving it one last grimace and a shudder. Then she turned back to Susannah, putting on her professional face. "Yeah, it's going great. They're on day two now, and it's a pretty big group this time. Ten volunteers…no, wait, eleven."

Susannah looked up. This was unusual. Rachel certainly had the authority to slip a latecomer into the training program without clearing it with her boss, but she didn't often do it. The volunteer application had a box for Susannah's signature, and Rachel wasn't comfortable with empty boxes.

Susannah wondered who the new recruit was. Nell Bollinger had been promising to sign up, but word was the Bollingers had just found pinkeye in their cattle, so this probably wasn't the week she'd finally decide to follow through.

"Eleven is excellent. Who is the new one? Do you remember her name?"

A stupid question, actually. Rachel was so detail oriented she undoubtedly knew the names, addresses, telephone numbers and shoe sizes of all eleven newbies by heart.

"Yes, of course! In fact, she said she was a friend of yours. Let's see. That one was Missy Griffin." She frowned slightly. "No, wait. She said she'd just gotten a divorce and gone back to her maiden name. Missy… Missy *Snowdon*. That's right."

Missy Snowdon…

Her chest suddenly tight, Susannah stared down at the telephone messages. She struggled to keep her face impassive.

Surely she'd heard wrong. Or else Rachel had remembered wrong.

For one thing, Missy Snowdon had left Texas years

ago. She'd gone to Hollywood, or maybe Vegas…one of those cities that act like magnets on women who are mostly made of collagen and silicone and bleach.

For another, Missy Snowdon wasn't the volunteering type. She was a player, not a worker. A taker, not a giver.

"Um…" Rachel tilted her head, obviously unsettled by something she saw in Susannah's face. "I hope I didn't do the wrong thing. I never would have let her sign up if she hadn't said she was your friend. If that's not true—"

"It's okay," Susannah said. "It's true. We were…we went to high school together."

She couldn't bring herself to speak the word *friends*. Once, she'd thought so, but…

As she'd said, Missy Snowdon was a taker. And what she'd taken from Susannah was Trent.

Rachel still looked worried, her brow furrowed. "Are you sure? The class is observing in Restorative this morning. I could go over and pull her out—"

"No, no, don't be silly. We don't have so many volunteers that we can afford to chase one away."

Rachel nodded. She knew what a struggle it was to fill the positions.

Susannah managed a smile. "I should get to these phone messages, I suppose. I can't stay long today."

"Oh, of course, what was I thinking? Call Dr. Grieve first. Then Mrs. McManus. Be sure to leave Des Barkley at the *Daily Grower* for last. He wants an interview about the peach party, which is good, but you know how he talks."

Susannah nodded. She knew.

It wasn't easy, but somehow she got through the

stack by noon. Some of it really was urgent. Some of it was downright boring. But at least it kept her mind off other things.

Like Trent.

And Missy Snowdon.

Susannah wished she'd had the nerve to ask Rachel how Missy looked. Back in high school, Missy had been the fairy princess, with a waterfall of blond hair and round, lash-heavy blue eyes. But the looks had been deceiving. Underneath all that innocent beauty beat the heart of a tiger.

For Missy Snowdon, a day without risk was a day without sunshine. She shoplifted trinkets she could easily afford, cheated on tests she was sure to ace anyhow. She ignored stop signs and streetlights, even when she had all the time in the world, gaily waving her beer can at every policeman she passed.

And boys…she could have had anyone in the school, from the greenest freshman to the married principal himself. But she had been picky. She wanted only the best. And only the ones who were already taken.

Like Trent.

Susannah tapped her pen against the calendar blotter. Finally, she stood up, unable to resist temptation any longer. Forget playing it cool. She had to see Missy for herself.

It would probably make her feel much better. Surely another decade of bleaching, boozing and bed-hopping had taken its toll. If there was any justice in this world, Missy probably looked a rode-hard fifty, and that would be a sight for sore eyes.

Susannah made her way to Restorative, passing from the relative quiet of the administrative wing to the noisy corridors of the clinic. Though she hurried, it was the lunch hour, and the trail was a bit of an obstacle course.

When she reached the small room where special restorative nurses were feeding the patients, she realized she was too late. The volunteers didn't hang out in any of the working areas. They would be intruding. They just stood to the side, observed quietly, then moved to a classroom for further discussion.

Darn. Susannah had lost her chance to do this the easy way. Of course, as the coordinator of volunteers, she had every right to poke her head into the training classroom and summon Missy Snowdon up for inspection any time she wanted. She had the power around here, not Missy. For once.

But she didn't want to use it. What would be the point? If she treated Missy badly, it would only prove that she still held a grudge, which would make her look pathetic. Their troubles had happened nearly eleven years ago, practically in another lifetime. They'd barely been out of high school, for heaven's sake. High school dramas had no power here, in the real world.

Just when she almost had herself convinced, a low, throaty laugh came from the west wing. The sound went right through her brave facade, like a dart busting a cheap balloon.

It had to be Missy. Because Susannah suddenly felt insecure and jealous and angry as hell.

She looked down the hall and saw a blond woman

moving toward her, flanked by two handsome, white-coated doctors who bent over her as solicitously as they would any critically ill patient in their care.

Susannah instinctively turned her head away, pretending to read a flyer at the nurses' station while the trio floated by, still laughing. She caught only a momentary flash of Missy, but that was enough.

Damn it. The woman was more beautiful than ever, still a princess in her candy-pink pinafore, still sashaying her hips as if she walked to secret salsa music. Still flashing the wide white smile that dazzled quarterbacks, traffic cops, algebra teachers—and apparently surgeons—into instant enslavement.

"Ms. Everly?" Evelyn Marks, the charge nurse, had returned to the station and sounded surprised to see Susannah standing there. That made sense. This wasn't Susannah's part of the building.

"Sorry…I mean *Mrs. Maxwell.*" Evelyn smiled. "I guess I gotta get used to that."

Susannah looked up just in time to see Missy and the doctors disappear onto the elevator. She turned to the nurse, who had been a casual friend for years. "Me, too, Evvy."

Evelyn, a bouncy, round mother of six daughters, three of whom were also nurses at the center, grinned. "You look tired. How's married life treating you?"

Susannah hesitated. But, like everyone else, Evvy knew the situation, so there was no point pretending to be a dewy-eyed bride.

"Well, it's…tricky," she admitted, opting for at least a degree of honesty.

Evvy laughed, but Susannah's ears were tuned to the tinkling sound as the elevator doors slid shut.

Missy was gone. For now. But even as Susannah breathed a sigh of relief, she knew she'd been a coward. And it was only a temporary reprieve. Sooner or later, she'd encounter her old nemesis face-to-face.

More importantly, so would Trent.

TRENT HAD his bulky work gloves on, and he'd just arranged the chain saw, pole pruner and baling cord under one arm and the old wooden paint ladder under the other, so naturally his cell phone chose that moment to ring.

He glanced back into the garage, where Zander was working on a broken hedge clipper.

The old man laughed. "Women," he said with a snort. "They have the devil's timing, don't they? Want me to tell Trixie Mae Sexpot to get lost for you?"

"Yeah. Thanks."

Trent wasn't expecting any calls from females, but he stood still as Zander reached into his jacket pocket and pulled out the phone. He would have let it go to voice mail, except that he was stealing these last few hours of daylight from the Double C and using them to cut back the worst dead branches on Everly's old oaks. If the Double C had a problem, he was honor bound to deal with it.

"Trent Maxwell's phone. Zander Hobbin speaking." Zander listened for a few seconds, during which his teasing expression soured into one of real annoyance.

"No, *Maxy* isn't available. You can tell by how he didn't answer the phone. See how that works, sugar?"

Trent felt his eyebrows draw together, and the chain saw slipped an inch under his elbow. *Maxy?* No one called him Maxy. Not anymore. Not since high school. And the only one who'd done it, even then, was...

"Who?" Zander cut a strange look toward Trent. "Missy Snowdon? Oh, you bet I remember you. Sure, I'll tell him. But just between you and me, don't hold your breath on that callback. Trent got married last week. You been gone a long time, so I'll just assume you didn't know, or you wouldn't have called, right?"

Trent could hear the high, quick voice still talking on the other end as Zander snapped the phone shut. The older man glowered at Trent from under his bushy eyebrows.

"I heard that little minx was back in town, but I didn't think she'd have the nerve to call you, just like that." He ran his upper lip through his teeth, as if he were trying to comb the mustache that tickled down over it. "Unless...you didn't make the first move, did you, son?"

Trent raised one eyebrow. That tone might have worked if Trent had been ten and had got caught with his hands in the wrong cookie jar, but not now. Trent wouldn't have telephoned Missy Snowdon if she were the last woman surviving this side of Saturn, but frankly, who he called or didn't call wasn't Zander's business.

"What's wrong, Zan? She *is* pretty hot. You jealous?"

Zander started to bluster, but he must have noticed the tucked corner of Trent's grin, because he ended up grunting and shaking his head.

"Jealous about Missy Snowdon? Hell, no. I wouldn't dream of going barefoot into that particular mud puddle." He slipped the phone back into Trent's jacket with two fingers, as if Missy Snowdon had infected it with something disgusting. "And neither should you, my friend. Neither should you."

"I don't go barefoot anywhere." Trent smiled. "Your generation might not have learned that, but ours has."

Zander grunted again, clearly aware he wasn't going to get anything but sardonic deflections, no matter how long he probed. Trent had mastered this technique in grade school. He could bat away Zander's curiosity all day long.

The two men were friendly colleagues, as managers of adjacent spreads tended to be, but they weren't confidants. Forty years stood between them, and so did Trent's natural preference for emotional privacy.

Zander slapped his hands against his overalls, raising dust in the sunbeams that angled into the dim garage like transparent gold two-by-fours. "So go on, then. Light's fading. Don't you have some limbs to cut?"

He did. It was one of many chores that desperately needed doing around here. He had been spending a lot of time at Everly over the past few days, ever since Harrison's weird warning about Peggy. He didn't really believe Peggy could pose a threat to anyone, but still… he didn't like the thought of Susannah here in this big old house, all alone.

Besides, the place could use an extra pair of hands, especially ones that came without a salary attached. He hadn't noticed just how run-down the place had become since old man Everly had died.

He propped his ladder up against the first oak. This one had a couple of dead branches that, given the right amount of wind, could easily fall right on the east porch roof. As he snapped the ladder's hinged stays into place, he noticed Eli Breslin over by the barn, slouching against the wall, staring at Trent.

Little bastard. He never did a lick of work around here, did he? He might as well be dipping his hand into Susannah's wallet and lifting out the cash.

"Hey, Breslin," Trent called. "If you're not busy, why don't you come cut some branches?"

Eli straightened, though the insolent look didn't drop from his face. He shook his head, the blond curls catching the late-afternoon sunlight. "Can't. Got to work on the shaker."

And then, as if he'd been planning all along to do so, he sauntered toward the back drive, where the old machine had been dragged yesterday after it died in the south forty. He glanced back at Trent, then picked up a wrench and proceeded to peer under the open hood.

Well, that was at least half an hour's work Susannah would get out of the brat today.

Trent went back to setting up his tools. Zander was right. The light was fading fast. He wouldn't get much done today. The older man had been right about another thing, too. Trent should have waited until he could have borrowed a good extension ladder from the Double C. Though Everly probably owned about a hundred ladders, they were all in use for the thinning, which would continue right up until harvest.

This old stepladder—the only one Susannah had kept

for private use—was a mess, with half-mangled feet that wouldn't settle level on the root-braided ground.

But the branches were his excuse for hanging around Everly this afternoon, so he needed to cut a few. Susannah would have laughed out loud if he'd admitted that Harrison Archer's comment had spooked him. She would have countered in her typical dry way that if she needed a guard dog, she'd buy one at the pound.

He looked toward the house. He could just barely make out Susannah's silhouette at the window of the sunroom. She'd been in there for a couple of hours now, going over estate details with Richard Doyle, the arrogant twit who was the executor of her grandfather's will.

Doyle might have been one of the reasons Trent had felt the need to stick around. Trent didn't like him, but that didn't mean much. Trent never liked guys like Doyle—guys who bought handkerchiefs to match their ties, which they'd bought to match their eyes, which they'd faked up with tinted contact lenses.

And he might as well be honest. He'd never liked any guy who dared to buzz around Susannah. It was habit, he supposed, but it clearly was a habit he wasn't going to break. Not after twenty-one years, ten with her and eleven without her. He was more likely to break the habit of breathing.

He wondered if she had the same problem. He wondered, for instance, how she would react to the news that Missy Snowdon had just called him.

Not that he planned to tell her. Missy's name was radioactive. It would burn his lips to say it and Susannah's ears to hear it. Maybe it wasn't fair. Missy wasn't to blame for their troubles—the tragedy had been Trent's fault, from beginning to end. But somehow Missy Snowdon had become more than just a trashy girl chasing another girl's man. She'd become iconic. A symbol.

Doves meant peace, rainbows meant hope, roses meant love.

Missy Snowdon meant betrayal and death.

He hadn't seen her in nearly a dozen years. He'd heard she was back in town, but, like Zander, Trent had assumed she'd know better than to call.

He and Susannah had little enough chance of making this marriage work without throwing Missy into the mix. You might as well dig up an old corpse, toss it onto the table, then ask everyone to enjoy their meal.

He bent over, set the choke on the chain saw. He gave the cord a yank, perhaps a little harder than necessary. Eli was watching him again, as if the boy hoped Trent would have trouble getting the tool started. But the chain saw zoomed into life, its teeth circling furiously, like a mad dog snapping, eager to chomp into something and tear it to shreds.

Trent climbed the ladder, careful not to ascend any higher than he needed to. Heights and chain saws didn't mix. But the limb was farther up than it appeared from the ground. Mildly irritated, he put one foot on the fourth step, then reached out with the chain saw and let it sink into the brittle, sapless limb.

The wood cracked, split and tumbled to the ground before the blade sank even halfway through it. It had been ready to go, that was for sure. He needed to get all this dead wood out of here before the summer storms started, even if it meant delegating some of the paper-work at the Double C.

He glanced at the tractor, just beyond the tree's branches. Eli was gone, the little slacker. Trent scanned the yard, his gaze ending at the back porch. He was sur-prised to see a man standing there. Would Eli really dare to—

But it wasn't Eli. It was Doyle. Dapper as ever, the lawyer posed like a *GQ* model, one foot cocked up against the white scrolled balustrade. His gold silk tie and handkerchief matched his hair.

Somebody should tell the fool that women didn't like their men to be prettier than they were.

Richard held a cocktail in his hand, a signal that the business part of his visit was over. Though Susannah must have provided the drink, she was nowhere in sight.

The porch was about twenty yards away, so it was hard to be sure, but the lawyer seemed to be staring up at the tree where Trent was working. And his handsome face seemed hard, set with hostile intensity that almost exactly replicated the anger Trent had glimpsed on Eli's face earlier.

Trent sighed. This could get old.

None of the men in Susannah's life trusted him. And they were jealous as hell. Okay, fair enough. He got that. The green-eyed monster wasn't exactly a stranger to him, either.

But too bad. Trent was her husband, at least for the next year, and all the wannabes, the sycophants and the stuffed shirts she'd passed over when making her choice would just have to deal with it.

Suddenly, Doyle raised his drink in a stiff salute.

"Afternoon, Maxwell," he called. He sipped the drink, then smiled. "Better watch your step up there."

"Yeah." Trent nodded. "Thanks." But he felt irrationally irritated. Naturally, Doyle thought cutting trees was dangerous. It was real physical labor, as foreign to the pencil pusher as scaling the craters of the moon.

Or was Trent just regressing again? Resenting the rich boys who never smelled like wood chips...or sweat?

Get over it, Maxwell, he told himself. That chip on his shoulder was every bit as pointless as Doyle's gold silk pocket square.

He held the chain saw above the next limb, then let it fall slowly, the blade slicing into the wood, sending off chips like sparks from a diamond cutter's wheel. But this branch wasn't completely dead. It resisted, and Trent had to put muscle behind it. He leaned over, adding his other foot to the fourth step for balance.

And suddenly, without any warning he could hear over the roar of the chain saw, the step gave way, the old bolt pulled away from the frame, and the plank jackknifed right under his feet.

As he felt himself go, he somehow had the presence of mind to release the chain saw. It died immediately and dropped, whining, like a missile to the ground.

The millisecond after, Trent's whole body did the same.

CHAPTER FIVE

IT WAS TWO IN THE MORNING. After a long evening poring through payroll records, Susannah yawned while she roamed the first floor, checking dead bolts and turning off lights.

As she passed the staircase that led down to the wine cellar, she heard a strange scrabbling noise deep in its shadows.

For a moment, she felt the hair on the back of her neck rise. The wine cellar had been her grandfather's last folly, a ridiculous expenditure better suited to the millionaire rancher he'd once been than the struggling, debt-ridden peach farmer he'd become.

She used the front part of the cellar now for preserves, and the occasional bottle of peach wine. The back half, beyond the wrought iron wine door, had become a mess of storage and clutter. Boxes of sentimental junk, yard games, canopies and chairs that came out only for parties, furniture too broken to sit in but too fine for the dump.

Her grandfather's ghost would be appalled.

Luckily, she didn't believe in ghosts.

But she heard the noise again, so it hadn't been her

imagination, either. It must be Trent down there, rooting around in the dark. She wondered why, then remembered that she'd mentioned she needed to dig out the tents and get them cleaned for the peach party.

She hadn't been hinting for him to do it. Had he thought she was? It wouldn't have crossed her mind to ask him to lug anything so heavy, not after taking that hard fall this afternoon.

She felt a nip, like a small bee sting of guilt, deep in her conscience. She hadn't even properly thanked him for his work on the trees, much less offered any TLC for his injury. Pitching in on odd jobs at Everly was above and beyond anything their "agreement" required of him. And things were such a mess around here that she was deeply grateful for any extra help from anyone.

She just hadn't known how to show it without feeling vulnerable. Only anger felt truly safe, and she hadn't had the courage to retreat from it, even when he clearly deserved better treatment.

Relations between them were obviously going to remain complicated, but that didn't absolve her from the obligation to show decent manners. She made her way down the stairs quickly. She had on only a nightshirt, but it was old and grubby, and no one could construe it as a come-on.

"Trent? Please don't bother with the tents tonight. They weigh a ton, and you shouldn't—"

To her surprise, he was sitting at the center tasting table, with a bottle of peach schnapps and a shot glass laid out before him on the recycled-wine-barrel surface. The recessed lighting her grandfather had installed overhead picked out blue-black diamonds in his hair, but the rest of him was mostly in shadow.

"Oh." She stopped at the foot of the stairs. "I'm sorry. I thought you might be trying to find the tents."

"No." He lifted the bottle and topped off the glass. "Just stealing a little home-made painkiller. If I took the stuff Doc Marchant left, I'd be a zombie tomorrow."

She glanced at his hand, which had a small bandage on the palm, and then his leg, which he had stretched out before him in an ever-so-slightly unnatural position. His jeans covered the cut on his calf, so she couldn't judge how bad it was.

"Does it hurt a lot?"

"Nothing the schnapps won't cure." He jiggled the bottle, sending little white fairy lights scampering over the brick walls. "This stuff packs a punch."

She knew it was true. When her grandfather had run out of money less than halfway through stocking these Malaysian mahogany racks, she'd found him down here almost every night, brooding over his laptop, researching wines he'd never buy and getting plastered on peach schnapps.

But although liquor had always made her grandfather meaner, it seemed to be mellowing Trent. His voice sounded almost warm, as if the drink famous for thawing out Alpine skiers had finally cut through the ice inside him, too.

"I heard Doc Marchant had to sew up your calf." She cringed, imagining. "Nineteen stitches, is that right?"

Trent shook his head. "That sounds like Zander's usual hyperbole. It was only six stitches, and only because Marchant is a worrywart. I've had worse cuts from sliding down rocks at Green Fern Pool."

She would have believed him, except that she'd seen the blood.

She still wasn't sure how it had happened. The memory had the disjointed quality of a nightmare. She'd just met Richard on the back porch when she heard the crash of something heavy and metallic slamming into the ground. And then, before she could identify the cause, she saw Trent tumble from the ladder.

Without thinking, she flew down onto the lawn, her heart racing. She called out his name. No pausing to consider her dignity. No wondering whether he'd want her help.

Pure reflex. Pure gut.

The ladder wasn't all that high, thank God, and it was clear immediately that there was no grave danger. While she knelt in the grass beside him, trying to still her heart and catch her breath, he pulled himself to his feet and shook himself off with a smile.

Within seconds, Zander, too, came running from the other side of the yard. The two men walked off together to check out what they insisted was just a scrape.

The message had been clear. Trent hadn't wanted her to fuss over him then, and he certainly wouldn't want it now.

"Well, I guess I should go," she said after an awkward pause. "I just wanted to be sure you weren't trying to haul out those tents. I was headed—"

She hesitated, suddenly uncomfortable about mentioning bed, for fear it might sound like an invitation. But the hesitation was conspicuous, too. "Headed upstairs."

He looked amused, though he didn't say anything.

Argh. She leaned her head against the cool bricks and shut her eyes for a second. Did every road lead to sex?

"I wanted to tell you…I'm really sorry about the ladder," she said, eager to change the subject. "As you can see, I've had to let a lot of the repairs and maintenance slide lately."

"Don't worry." He smiled. "I won't sue."

She couldn't help smiling back. "That's only because you know there's nothing to get."

He raised one eyebrow, toying with his empty shot glass with the tips of his fingers. "Oh, I wouldn't say that. No *money,* maybe."

The cellar's extravagant, Internet-monitored thermostat and humidity control system had long ago been disabled, but suddenly the temperature in the shadowy room seemed to drop ten degrees. Susannah looked at his fingers, and something about their slow grace made her shiver.

The way he looked at her…

There was no mistaking what he meant.

Suddenly she realized what a foolish mistake she'd made, letting guilt send her down here. She knew he hadn't given up his plan to make her pay, and wasn't this the perfect spot, with its cool seclusion, the musty smell of old wine and the sticky sweet scent of peaches? He must have known she'd come. He'd waited here, like a panther, in the dark.

And she'd fallen right into the trap. She was the moronic horror movie heroine who, even knowing there was a killer in the house, still decided to investigate the spooky noises in the basement.

"But then," he went on, "money hasn't ever been my weakness."

His voice made her shiver, too. She crossed her arms in front, holding them by the elbows, trying to warm herself. "Trent, I really should go to—"

"To bed. Yes, I know. We can do that, too, if you like. Later."

"That isn't what I meant. You're deliberately mis-understanding me."

"I think we understand each other perfectly." He held out a hand, palm up. The bandage gleamed in the recessed lights. "You made a bargain, and it's time to keep it. I promise you it won't be too painful. It will meet all your terms, Sue. All pleasure. No risk. No repercussions."

She flushed, well aware of what he wanted. Oral sex. He wanted her to take him into her mouth, and her hands, and make him come. Back when they first made love, at only eighteen, he'd begged her to. He'd told her that all girls did it. All men wanted it.

But she'd been afraid, afraid that she wouldn't know how, that she wouldn't be good enough, that she'd try and try, humiliating herself, only to fail.

She'd been such a prissy lover, she knew that now. Such a tame little Puritan. Only in the back of the car, only with their clothes on, only on the bottom, only in the dark.

She'd been so naive, in fact, that when she stumbled on Trent and Missy Snowdon in the abandoned playground that rainy midnight, sitting together on the swing, she had no idea what was happening.

She hadn't been able to see him all day. Her grandfather had company and he required her to be on hostess duty. Trent, of course, hadn't been invited. By late night, she knew that Trent probably wasn't expecting her to show up at the playground, where they sometimes met. But she sneaked out anyhow, hoping against hope that he might have gone there, too, just in case. Surely he wanted to see her as much as she wanted to see him.

The sound reached her first, the grind of metal against metal as someone pumped the swing rhythmically back and forth. She heard throaty laughter, and other noises that were harder to identify.

She peered toward the swing set, off in a corner. Rain diamonds winked as moonlight caught on the metal legs and the thick, glistening rod of the frame. She saw the groaning swing move back and forth, never going very high, two sets of hands gripping the wet chains, slipping, gripping again.

At first she thought they were just playing. Doubled up, with Missy in Trent's lap, the way children might do just for the crazy fun of flying backward. Limbs tangled, hair flying, sharing the thrill.

Shock made her stupid. She worried, like an idiot, whether the chains were strong enough to hold them both, with Trent so tall, so much heavier than any child.

But then Missy's groans turned to soft screams, and the swing's rhythm became jerky, spasming as Trent's heels dug into the ground, finding traction to push harder, thrust faster, finding his own orgasm there in the rain.

And then, finally, far, far too late, Susannah understood. Understood that he had needed more than an uptight little prude.

That she wasn't enough for him.

That the world as she knew it was over.

She wondered why the memory still hurt so much, when she'd hardly thought of that night in years.

Was it because she was finally old enough to see what an idiot she'd been to run away that night, scalded, to nurse her wounds in private and concoct a revenge plot as stupid as flirting with Paul? She knew now that she should have charged right up to that swing set and overturned the cheating bastard headfirst into the dirt. Even if she'd scratched Missy Snowdon's eyes out, that would have been a more mature way to handle it. It couldn't have saved their relationship, but it might have saved Paul's life.

Or maybe the memory felt so fresh and raw again because she realized that she owed Trent. She had made a deal with him, and he'd kept his part of the bargain. After all these years, she was going to have to live up to her part of their agreement and let him touch her again…something he hadn't done since that night.

"All right," she said in a low voice. "I'll give you what you want. But only because I know you, and I know that if you don't get what you need here, you'll go looking for it somewhere else."

He didn't answer. He just sat there, waiting, as if he didn't care what her reasons were. The king, waiting for his subject to perform.

She felt something harden inside her. She crossed the

marble floor in five steps. He still sat in the chair, with his leg stretched out at that odd angle. She took a breath, then, holding the arms of his chair for stability, she sank to her knees in front of him.

"I'll do it, because I won't be a laughingstock for you again."

He smiled oddly. "And because you promised this would be a real marriage? Because you used that promise to get me to marry you? Because you wouldn't want to be a liar and a fraud?"

She tilted her head up and met his gaze without flinching. "You're right. I made this deal, and I have to live with it. But I want you to know that I hate you. I hate you for not being man enough to set me free."

He tilted his head an inch to one side, though otherwise he didn't move a muscle. "I'm afraid you'll have to hate me, then."

She nodded, understanding that there was to be no reprieve. She reached out, forcing her hands not to tremble, and carefully unbuckled his belt. She felt him watching her, but she didn't raise her eyes to his face again.

She unbuttoned the top of his jeans, and as her hands grazed the denim she felt the heat rising from him. She sensed the swollen bulk of his penis under the cloth. Instinctively, she cupped it with her palm, as a sudden tactile memory burned through her.

She had thought this would be strange, after all these years, after all the anger. But though their hearts had grown apart, grown bitter, their bodies were still the same. This was still Trent, her Trent. She knew him. She knew what he felt like, the shape and warmth and musky smell of him.

He pulsed under her hand. He needed this. She remembered how he had always looked as he first thrust into her, an agony of tension and heat, as if his body was on fire, and only she could put out the flames. It had thrilled her, but it had scared her, too, because she sensed a power she couldn't control.

She slid the zipper down one millimeter at a time, knowing that the pressure was dragging along the length of him like a slow torture. When it was fully open, she pulled back the edges of the denim, slid her hand under the cotton boxers, and took the hard fullness of him into her hand.

He groaned. He throbbed once under her fingers, and she was shocked to realize that something hot and deep inside her was throbbing, too.

She wanted this. For the first time in her life she desperately wanted to feel this velvet steel against her teeth, her tongue. Her mouth curved, instinctively knowing what to do.

She bent her head. But then, out of nowhere, his hands were against her hair.

"What?" His voice was hoarse. "No foreplay?"

She drew a jagged breath. She looked up at him, feeling slightly dazed. Frustration coursed through her. She was ready. He was ready.

"What do you mean, foreplay?"

He rose to his feet in one graceful motion, his hands urging her up along with him. Before she could orient herself, he held her buttocks and lifted her onto the table.

"I mean this," he said. He slid his hand under her nightshirt and eased off the panties she wore beneath.

He tossed the bit of silk onto the floor and then returned to her, running his rough hands up the length of her thighs. Her knees fell apart, as if they were marionette legs controlled by invisible strings. He went without hesitation to the aching, moist spot he knew so well, and with perfect confidence began to stroke, and press and circle.

She grabbed his shoulders, weak and suddenly dizzy. His fingers were hot, and she was hot, and it felt wonderful and dangerous. It took her breath away.

"Trent," she said, though the word sounded as if it came out on a choke.

He gazed down at her. She wondered whether she looked as dazed as she felt. He smiled cryptically, and then he bent his head and kissed her on her lips. The touch was sweet and lingering, a strange contrast to the hot domination of his fingers.

"It's all right, Susannah," he whispered. "Don't fight it. Lean back."

His voice alone controlled her. The cool cork somehow met her back, though her hips were half on, half off the table, her legs dangling helplessly over the edge.

But he took her feet, and gently rested her legs across his shoulders. He carried her, braced her, and she was completely open to him. It felt so right, strangely safe, and her hips began to move on the table, shifting slightly, responding to his fingers.

And then, when she could hardly think, it wasn't his fingers anymore. It was his mouth, and his tongue and tiny, fiery hints of teeth. And then came dark heat, and the softest, coaxing pull.

He'd never done this to her, no one had ever done it, but it was perfect, like watching fireworks from a river, like being the fireworks and being the river, like pushing and pulling, like coiling and burning, and burning…

And finally the explosion that somehow she knew she had been born for.

When it stopped, she had no idea how long she lay there. She wasn't sure she'd ever breathe normally again, or sit up or speak. But somehow, little by little, her heart subsided to normal, and she felt reality gathering around her.

She sensed movement, and when she opened her eyes, Trent was sorting out her nightshirt, pulling it down over her thighs. He carefully eased her legs down so that her feet just barely touched the floor.

With one firm hand behind her shoulder, he nudged her to a sitting position.

And then he began to buckle his belt.

"Trent." She stared at the belt, unable to meet his eyes. "I thought—"

She felt like a child just learning to speak. Her mouth wouldn't move quite right, and words eluded her.

She watched his cool motions as he pulled himself together and headed for the cellar stairs.

"Good night, Sue."

He looked so…unmoved. If his lips weren't slightly swollen, she would think she had imagined the entire experience.

"Trent…"

He turned. "Yes?"

"That's all? You're leaving?"

He tilted his watch. "It's late. I have to be at the Double C by six."

Though she wished she could think of something sharp to say, her mind still felt too scrambled. "But I thought you—I thought you wanted me to—"

"I guess you thought wrong, Susannah." He smiled, the classic Trent Maxwell mocking grin. "It wouldn't be the first time."

FROM THE WINDOW of his office at the Double C the next morning, Trent watched Alcatraz taking a spin around the paddock.

Trent was supposed to be checking over payroll records, but he'd never been crazy about the paperwork part of his job. Right now he couldn't take his eyes off the potent combination of sunshine, magnificent quarter horse and wide green pastures.

The scene called to him, making his office feel small and stuffy, his work pointless.

But who was he kidding? This mood hadn't come over him because his work was dull. The Double C had twenty-five thousand acres for him to patrol, a million issues to deal with—both indoors and out—and a stable of ranch horses to ride whenever he wanted.

No, this itchy dissatisfaction was all about Susannah.

He tapped his foot against the wooden floor and added a syncopated rhythm with his pen. He couldn't stop thinking about last night—and wondering whether he'd made a serious mistake.

She wouldn't lightly forgive him for the episode in the cellar. He knew that—he'd known even before he touched her that he'd pay dearly for it.

Susannah had always been a proud woman, determined to be in control of her life, her heart…and her body. Even back when they were in the throes of young love, she'd been self-conscious about the final moment of physical surrender. Today, when she saw him as the enemy, and sex as the battleground, that complete meltdown must have felt like a humiliating defeat.

It had begun as a power trip, he had to admit that. He'd wanted to show her that she wasn't as indifferent as she pretended to be. He had wanted to force her to admit that she still felt something for him.

But, in the end, the simple desire to touch her, and taste her, had been overpowering. He'd needed that more than he'd needed his own release.

Not that the victory had exactly been an ego boost. Making her catch fire had been about as difficult as setting a match to dry kindling. She'd been ready. Beyond ready. Any man who had touched that pent-up dynamite would have created a similar explosion.

Maybe he should have let her finish what she'd started out to do. If she'd been able to control him, to decide what he'd feel and when, she might have been less resentful. He certainly would have been less frustrated.

Trent unbuttoned his cuffs and rolled back his sleeves, wondering if the air conditioner might be broken. He had to get out of here.

It wasn't about the urge to find Susannah and stage a repeat of last night.

It wasn't. He just needed some air....

Luckily, before he could stand up, the door opened and Chase entered, looking dusty and tired.

Trent settled back into his chair. *Saved by the boss.*

"We found Blue Boy," Chase said without preamble. The two men were such old friends that they'd long ago dispensed with formalities. Besides, Trent knew all about the missing horse.

"Where was he?"

"The rascal found a bad piece of fencing out by the west ridge and jumped it."

"Is he okay?"

Chase dropped onto the comfortable chair opposite the desk and put his feet up with a sigh. "He twisted his right hind leg. Doc says it's a tendon, not too bad, luckily, so he'll recover. Out of commission for a while, though."

Trent shook his head. "Wish I thought it would teach Blue a lesson. He's too old to go gallivanting."

Chase chuckled. "No such thing, pal. At least I hope there isn't." He yawned happily and scratched at a grass stain on his shirt. Chase was a true Texas blue blood, fifth-generation millionaire, but he loved to get dirty, sneaking away from black tie events to tackle work even his ranch hands hated.

"So. I hear you took a tumble yourself." Chase lifted his chin, pretending to try to see over the edge of the desk. "Clumsy bastard. How hard is it to stay upright on a ladder?"

"Depends on the ladder," Trent said with a scowl. "Everything she's got over there needs fixing. This one was about a hundred years old. The step just gave out under me."

"That damn girl's too proud to live." Chase dusted the knee of his jeans, sending a little cloud of gray Double C dirt into the air. "She can't ask me to loan her a ladder? She lets her people climb around on a rusted piece of crap?"

"Well…" Trent toyed with his pen. "That's the weird thing."

Suddenly, Chase's yawning, sleepy-eyed manner disappeared. He knew Trent, and he recognized the tone.

"What weird thing?"

"I'm not sure. At first I just assumed, as you did, that the bolts were rotten. But I got to thinking, and I'm not so sure. The ladder fell right beside me, and I was lying there a second or two, staring straight at it."

"And?"

"I didn't really put two and two together at the time, being preoccupied with making sure all my body parts still worked. But now that I think back, I'm pretty sure I didn't see any rust."

Chase frowned. "That doesn't make sense. You mean the break was clean?"

"Yeah. Straight. As if someone had cut it in two."

"Did you go back and take a second look at the ladder?"

"It's gone. Zander said Susannah had told him to get rid of it ASAP, so he got Eli to shove it into the Dumpster. They already picked it up. They compact it on the spot, you know. That ladder's history."

"That *is* weird." Chase was quiet a moment. "Anybody else know you were going up to cut branches that day?"

Trent tried to remember who might have heard. He'd mentioned it several times over the past few days. He'd kept meaning to do it, but he kept getting sidetracked.

"Zander knew. And Eli, I guess. And probably that obnoxious Richard Doyle. He's been at the house three mornings in a row, sucking up to Sue, though he says it's about the will."

Chase nodded. "And Sue."

Trent narrowed his eyes. "What?"

"Sue." Chase shrugged. "I'm just saying, if you think Doyle knew, then Sue must have told him. So Sue must have known, too."

Trent decided to ignore that. Chase had played Sherlock Holmes recently, trying to discover the true identity of Josie's baby's father, and his success must have gone to his head.

He actually thought Sue might have sabotaged her own ladder?

Some detective.

"Obviously she had opportunity, but still, she did marry you only a week ago." The corners of Chase's eyes tilted up. "You're an irritating son of a gun, but even you couldn't have turned her homicidal in a week."

Trent laughed, glad to see that Chase was just joking. "I don't know. Guess it depends on what old man Everly's will says about widows."

He glanced out the window again, as the trainer led Alcatraz back to the stables. What a gorgeous horse he was. He'd been sired by Chase's father's favorite quarter horse, Rampage, a stallion who had definitely lived up to his name. The only one of the Fugitive Four who had been allowed to ride Rampage had been Paul, who'd had such a light hand on the reins and whose intuition about horses had been almost perfect.

"Oh. That reminds me. When I visited Peggy Archer last week, I think I mentioned to her that I'd be cutting back some branches at Everly. Not that I'm implying…"

He paused, remembering. "It was a strange visit, Chase. Harrison actually took me outside and warned me about Peggy. Said a lot of bad feelings got stirred up when Susannah and I got married."

Chase nodded again. "I can imagine. We're all married now…something Paul will never get a chance to do. That's gotta be tough. Still…it's kind of hard to picture Peggy Archer sneaking into Sue's barn with a hacksaw, don't you think?"

"Impossible. Till she gets that new hip, Peggy can barely walk from the chair to the door."

"So…"

They sat in silence a minute, considering the possibilities—which were, in the end, all impossible. The bottom line was, no one could have known that Trent would use that particular ladder on that particular day.

Finally Chase sighed. "Sorry, pal, it's just too nuts. Nobody's out to get you. You must have been imagining things."

"Possibly. I *had* just hit my head against an oak root the size of a water main."

"Clumsy bastard," Chase repeated affectionately. "Still, women love an injured warrior. I hope you at least have the sense to milk those stitches for a little pity sex."

"*Pity* sex?" Trent laughed out loud. "For God's sake, Chase. How desperate do you think I am?"

"On a scale of one to ten?" Grinning, Chase stood up and headed for the door. "I'd say about a thousand."

CHAPTER SIX

NEWLYWEDS, Trent decided as he watched Chase and Josie try to assemble the new crib, were disgusting. They should be locked up for the first full calendar year, so they didn't drive everyone else crazy with their cuddles and kisses and lingering looks of hungry adoration.

Of course, technically Trent and Susannah were newlyweds, too. But that was different. Night and day different.

It was a bright Sunday afternoon, the last weekend in May, and the two couples had been working on the nursery at the Double C for the past two hours. Well, at least Trent and Susannah had been working. Chase and Josie got very little done, seemingly magnetized to one another. Chase couldn't pass within six feet of his new wife without scooping her into his arms for a cuddle. Josie couldn't hand him the screwdriver without ending up kissing his neck.

Susannah and Trent, on the other hand, seemed to exist in two separate universes, even when they were standing mere inches apart. In the past two hours, Susannah had met Trent's eyes only once, the moment he arrived. Her shock had been almost palpable. She obviously hadn't realized, when she agreed to help Josie today, that it would be a double date.

Trent had glanced at Chase. *Good try, pal,* he'd messaged silently. Chase had shrugged, his smile not admitting anything.

Though Susannah was clearly unhappy about the arrangement, she couldn't be accused of being rude. She worked hard. She laughed at Chase's jokes, and oohed over Josie's fluffy lamb mobiles and lamb border stencils and lamb-patterned sheets.

It was only Trent who got the invisible man treatment. She talked around him, walked around him, worked around him without skipping a beat.

"Hey, guys. Would you mind working on the stencil border while we assemble the mobile?" Chase wrapped one arm around Josie's waist. "I don't want Josie in here with the paint fumes. Not good for the baby."

Trent gazed over at Susannah, who frowned. He wondered how she was going to get out of this one.

"Do you really think that needs to be done today?" She smiled to soften the words. "The baby's not due till mid-September, and it's not even June yet."

Trent felt her frustration. Back at Everly, peaches were ripening on the trees in record numbers. She'd spent every day of the past month trying to line up buyers. Tomorrow the harvest would begin, with its harrowing fourteen-hour days. Susannah wouldn't have another free Sunday until late August.

Josie grinned, unabashed. "I know. But I just can't wait to see it. I'm so grateful that you guys are willing to help. It means so much to both of us."

Trent glanced at Chase, who beamed and planted a kiss on the top of her head, as if she'd said something marvelous.

Man, the guy was *gone* on his wife. He clearly didn't know how to deny her anything. If she'd wanted the baby's room decorated in angel feathers and bits of the pearly gates, Chase would have driven his truck up to Heaven's door and demanded they sell him some.

"Okay, then, we'll be in the study if you need us." Chase apparently had decided to take Susannah's silence as a yes. That was absurd, of course. Chase had been Susannah's best friend since they were babies, and he knew as well as Trent what her frozen face really meant. "Have fun."

They ambled off, still entwined, still teasing each other, still making silly kissing noises between sentences. When they finally disappeared, Trent turned to Susannah with a smile.

"Wow. You could get cavities, just being in the same room with all that sugar."

She didn't smile back. "I think it's sweet."

"My point exactly. Sweet like six banana splits and a double hot fudge sundae. Stomachache sweet."

She studied the stencil. "They're happy. That's what marriage is all about. Most marriages, anyhow." She turned and held the stencil up against the wall, studying it. "I think it's great."

Well, of course she did. Whatever Trent thought, she thought the opposite. If he said *go*, she'd stop. If he said *silence* she'd sing.

If he said, *Come here, Sue, because I want to make love to you until you forget how to be such a bitch...*

She'd run.

And, obviously, neither of them would ever forget that this should have been their own sugary bliss. The look in Susannah's eyes said it all. If Trent hadn't cheated on her, they would have been the kissing, cooing newly-weds.

She had wanted that, once. Trent knew it had been her most comforting dream. It had helped her endure the loss of her parents, and her grandfather's brutality.

And he'd killed it.

She would never forgive him for that. Hell, he'd never forgive himself.

But life went on, damn it. Why couldn't she let go of the past long enough to get through this year without adding more misery to the heaping load they already carried around?

"So let's see how this works." He plucked the stencil from her fingers. "Ummm..." He turned it in all directions, trying to figure out how exactly this collection of random slits in a wobbly plastic rectangle was going to end up looking like anything. "Sorry, but...what the *hell?*"

In spite of her obvious belief that cracking a smile in his presence would usher in the end of the world, he saw the corner of her mouth tuck back.

"It's a simple stencil, really. Just one color, just one layer. See? You press the stencil against the wall, then sponge over it with paint. What comes through will look like a lamb."

"Really." He squinted. *It would,* he thought, *probably help to be drunk.* "I'll have to take your word for it."

But she didn't seem to be listening anymore. When he glanced toward her, he was rewarded with a close-up of her tight, round ass. She'd bent over and begun squeezing blobs of white acrylic paint onto the plates that waited on the bright blue drop cloth.

He took a minute to enjoy the sight. Expecting to work hard—and definitely *not* expecting to see Trent— she'd dressed casually today. Instead of her regular tailored khaki slacks and oxford cloth shirt, she was wearing cutoff blue jeans, frayed up to the danger zone, and a tiny white halter top.

Eleven years ago, he would have grabbed her in both hands and pulled her in for an X-rated squeeze that would have put Chase and Josie to shame. They would have ended up laughing, stumbling and probably covered in white paint.

Today, they lived under new laws. He gave himself that one stolen minute to look, and then turned away before she sensed the heat of his gaze.

"The border goes along the edge of the ceiling, I suppose?" There were still two ladders in the room, from when Trent and Chase had painted the baby-blue walls two weeks ago, and they'd obviously been left for a reason.

She stood on tiptoe to investigate. "Yeah. Chase already drew the guidelines, so we don't have to worry about spacing. You can start over by the closet. I'll start by the door."

Her gaze dropped to his calf, which still had a bandage over Marchant's six stitches. "Unless…" She waved toward the injury. "If you'd rather not…"

He laughed. "You think I've developed a fear of ladders?"

"Probably not." She actually smiled at that.

For about twenty minutes they worked in silence, atop their own perches on opposite sides of the room. He taped the stencil in place, sponged the paint onto the wall, then moved the stencil and began again.

The lambs looked blobby…. Was he using too much paint? His hands felt too big, mostly thumbs. Though he'd done only five lambs, he was already bored.

He glanced back to see how her wall was coming.

Far better than his, naturally. She had so much more control, so much more patience. He was restless, physical, more comfortable outdoors. He'd always marveled at her ability to sit quietly, to wait, to think things through, to stay on task.

He had none of that. Which was, of course, why he'd botched up his life for so long, making one impulsive mistake after another. What patience he had acquired had come at great cost…and it still didn't come naturally.

He climbed down, moved his ladder and filled his plate with white paint. He climbed up again, ignoring the twinge in his stitches, and taped the stencil in place. Just before he touched the sponge to the wall, he noticed that he'd taped the lamb upside down.

In spite of his annoyance, he had to laugh. Josie was going to regret letting him get involved with this. "Hey.

Remember when Nikki decided she wanted unicorns all over her walls?"

He wasn't surprised when Susannah didn't immediately answer. Normally, they avoided "Remember when" as a conversation starter. But he'd spoken without thinking, of course. And besides, damn it, he was tired of pretending that ten years of intimacy and fun hadn't existed, just because they'd ended in one night of disaster.

She must have decided the same thing, because after only a brief hesitation, she chuckled, too.

"I hope that doesn't mean what I think it means." She put down her sponge and twisted her head to see his border. "Have you screwed up already?"

"Yeah. I almost put one on upside down." He leaned back to let her get a full view of the mess. "Is the paint supposed to drip like that? My lambs look sort of... deformed."

She frowned, studying his line of white, puffy animals. "It's not too bad," she said finally. "You're using too much paint, that's all. I can probably go back with the blue and touch it up."

"Oh." He stared at his row of lambs, as if they'd betrayed him. "Darn."

"*Darn?* You wanted me to say they were awful?"

"Yeah." He grinned. "I was hoping you'd order me to surrender my sponge immediately."

"Nope." She dabbed her own sponge into the white paint. "Sorry. And don't go making it worse deliberately, just to get out of it. It didn't work with the unicorns, did it?"

It certainly hadn't. At five, Nikki had been in love with unicorns, and she'd begged Susannah, Trent, Paul and Chase—who, at nineteen, still called themselves the Fugitive Four—to paint the creatures on her bedroom walls.

Ever sensible, Susannah found a picture to copy, but unfortunately none of the boys had an iota of artistic talent. Trent's contributions were the worst, looking like everything from rhinos to car keys…but never like unicorns.

Nikki, who at the time was crazy about Trent, adored the weird creations. She egged him on, encouraging him to make them ever wilder, despite Susannah's frustrated efforts to keep everyone copying the pattern.

Chase and Paul joined in the fun, abandoning the original design without regret. It took a while, but by the end of the day even Sue relented and began adding inventive flourishes to her unicorns, too.

The result was colorful madness, but it had been so joyous, a visible representation of the love and creative camaraderie that had existed among the four friends. It had been one of their happiest days.

They'd all been crushed when, two days later, Arlington Everly had sent one of the ranch hands up to paint over it with a bland eggshell white. It had taken four coats to cover it all, which had given them an irrational sense of pride.

"Okay, but if my lambs all look like unicorns, let it be on your head." He tapped the sponge against the edge of the plate, making sure it didn't soak up too much paint. "That was a fun day, wasn't it?"

He didn't look at Susannah, but he could feel her

tension all the way across the room. He could almost hear her thoughts. She was trying to calculate risk, vulnerability, exposure. Was it too dangerous to agree that yes, she, too, remembered that day with pleasure? Was she somehow in danger if she admitted that, on that one day, they had been happy?

"Yes," she said finally. "Yes, it was a beautiful day."

He waited, wondering whether she'd find a way to erase the tenderness with an extra comment. *A great day, and isn't it too bad that you had to go and spoil it all? A great day, but only because we didn't know how soon Paul would be dead.*

She didn't. The gentle sound of her "yes" hung in the air, untouched. When he looked up, she had already gone back to swabbing the stencil with her sponge.

It wasn't much. But somehow it felt like a victory.

Suddenly Josie came into the room, holding Trent's cell phone in one outstretched hand. She crossed the room quickly and stopped at the foot of his ladder.

"It must have fallen off when you and Chase were assembling the bookcase," she said. "It was ringing, so I answered it for you. It's Missy Snowdon? She said it was urgent."

Chase appeared in the doorway, holding the fuzzy pieces of the mobile he'd obviously been putting together. The look on his face was priceless. Josie's hand wavered, as if she realized she'd goofed, though she wasn't sure how.

Trent had to enjoy the irony. Though Chase must have told Josie at least some details of Trent and Susannah's problems, apparently he had withheld the piece about Trent sleeping with Missy Snowdon. To protect Trent's reputation, no doubt.

What a joke. Once again, fate proved that hiding the truth didn't work. Secrets simply wouldn't stay buried.

He took the telephone, because, in the end, what else could he do?

He glanced once at Susannah.

He shouldn't have.

"Hello, Missy," he said in an even tone. "Is everything all right?"

"Not really," her arch, sexy voice responded. "My old friend Maxy isn't answering my calls or returning my messages. Here I am, between love affairs and between cocktails, just looking to get together with an old friend, and he won't give me the time of day. I can't figure out why that would be. Can you?"

"It's pretty simple." Trent watched Susannah's face, which had hardened into a sardonic indifference that he was pretty sure he recognized. Had she learned that look from him? "I don't know if you heard. I just got married."

"Oh, I heard. Everyone's talking about it. But it's not *that* kind of marriage, is it? Word on the street is that she still hates your guts. Sounds like you need a little TLC just as much as I do. And by TLC I mean, touching, licking—"

"Missy." God almighty. She was drunk, and it was only, what…about three in the afternoon? Poor, beautiful Missy Snowdon. He could have predicted she'd find the real world to be so much harder than high school.

Pity softened his voice. "I'm sorry, but I'm not

going to be able to help you with that. But it was nice of you to call."

Susannah made a low, disgusted noise. She dropped her sponge in the paint, wiped her hands on her shorts, and began backing down the ladder.

"Come on, Maxy," Missy wheedled. "I hear she won't sleep with you, even though she promised she would. And I know you. You can't go a year—"

"I'm sorry, but I'm just not available right now. It was good to talk to you. Take care of yourself."

He flipped the phone shut, though she kept talking. He wondered if, when she realized he was gone, she'd call right back. Just in case, he turned the phone to silent mode.

He looked at Susannah, who was watching him, as rigid as an ice mannequin. She smiled slightly, as if she found his predicament amusing, but the frost in her eyes said something different.

Without warning, anger bubbled up, like a geyser that had been dormant so long he'd almost forgotten it was there.

Was it his fault Missy Snowdon needed a man and had decided to become Trent's own personal stalker? He hadn't touched the redhead in almost eleven years, for God's sake. Was there no such thing as forgiveness? No Get Out of Jail card in the game of Susannah Everly's life?

He was a bloody fool. Why was he trying to make this goddamn marriage work? She wasn't ever going to forgive him. She wasn't ever going to forget. Maybe, over the years, she'd lost whatever sweetness and humanity she'd once possessed.

And if she had nothing to offer him but ice and hatred, why the hell shouldn't he take what Missy Snowdon had to offer? He was tired of guilt, tired of loneliness, tired of wearing sackcloth and ashes while he beat his fists against Susannah's locked door.

Missy might be a drunk, but at least she wasn't a walking textbook of resentment, repression and every emotional issue known to man.

And she got pleasure from making a man feel good, not out of making him feel like shit.

He glanced at the phone, thinking how good it would feel to thumb it open and hit Redial, right here, while Susannah watched with that supercilious look on her face. That "I know you're a bastard" look, which, paradoxically, just made him want to prove her right.

"Trent." Chase's voice cut into his thoughts. "Pal. Think it through."

Trent glanced up. Chase looked worried, but steady. No pressure, which he knew from long experience wouldn't work with Trent at a moment like this. Just a reminder that sanity was still an option.

It was a look that had stopped Trent from doing a lot of dumb things through the years.

Trent took a breath. Then he slowly slid the cell phone into his back pocket.

He glanced toward Susannah, wondering if she knew how close he'd come.

But she had already left the room.

CHAPTER SEVEN

SOMETIMES, life just didn't seem fair.

The next day, in the silver-pink early-morning sunlight, Susannah stood at the edge of her two-acre rows of Rio Grande trees, the first of her peaches to ripen.

She tried not to feel bitter about the rotten trick fate had played on her.

For the first year she could remember, Everly's orchards had been blessed with perfect conditions. No frost, no drought, no catfacing, no scab. As a result, thousands of juicy peaches hung from the trees like Christmas ornaments, glowing gold with deep red blush, throwing off waves of mouthwatering sweetness.

But unless she could pull off a miracle, much of this beautiful fruit would rot, unsold, in cold storage. Because this year, this perfect year, was also the year her biggest buyer had gone bankrupt. The other retail outlets were already contracted with other growers.

Except for a few little mom-and-pop stores, and a bunch of roadside stands, she had nowhere to sell her crop.

Zander came up beside her, panting, his bulky form already sweating, though a chill still hung in the air. It was that kind of morning, when no one moved slowly. Every morning for the next three months would be like that.

"Snap out of it," he said, handing her one of the drop-bottom bags. "Feeling sorry for yourself isn't going to get the peaches picked."

"I know. But look at those trees. They're *all* going to look like that this year, from the Rios to the Dixie-lands. All five hundred acres, all twenty-five varieties. What are we going to do if a new bulk buyer doesn't show up in the next few weeks?"

He shook his head. "Beats me. Right now all I care about is getting this fruit off the trees. You going to help me or not?"

She smiled. "Yes, sir."

Adjusting her hat and squaring her shoulders, she scanned the workers, who were pouring out of the makeshift office, where they'd been issued their gear. Male and female, old and young, they began to filter into the rows of dawn-lit trees, ladders and bushel baskets in hand, laughing and talking.

By the time the sun hit the treetops, Susannah knew, only the superfit would still be laughing. The rest would be sweating and silent, aching from shoulder to toe.

Most of her workers each season were regulars, college students and teachers on summer vacation, as well as whole families of migrants who knew the rhythms of nature so well they magically appeared the day she needed them.

But this year she'd hired at least thirty extra pickers to cope with the bumper crop. Many of them were newbies and would need a lot of supervision, just to be sure they didn't manhandle the fruit or pack it so deep she ended up with box after box of peach mush.

Where the peaches would go after they'd been picked and packed, Susannah had no idea. She was still making calls, exploring options, searching her brain for new ideas, but mostly she was just praying for a miracle. She even dreamed once that a new grocery chain began building a store downtown. In her dream, she'd grabbed a hammer and nails and joyously leaped on a scaffold to help.

She watched the workers, eager to begin, none of them wondering where it would end. "Do you think maybe we could add another couple of roadside stands?"

"We've already doubled what we had last year." Zander tucked his thumbs into his belt loops and sighed. "I did as you said and got Eli supervising the deliveries to the roadside stands. Trent offered to oversee the pick-your-own acres."

Susannah shot him a hard look. "Shouldn't Trent be at the Double C?"

Zander shrugged. "He said he could spare the time."

"Still, he doesn't know anything about peaches—"

"Ms. Susannah, follow my logic. He offered. We need him. I said yes."

Her chest tightened. Though Zander was right, she was reluctant to take any favors from Trent. She didn't want to owe him any more than she already did.

Plus, just knowing he was around would be distracting. They hadn't spoken since yesterday afternoon, when Missy had called him at the Double C. He had come straight home after finishing up in the nursery. It had been a difficult day, just spending so many hours around Chase and Josie. Susannah was happy for them, really she was. But their uninhibited joy made her think about things that were better left forgotten.

Things like how, once upon a time, she'd truly believed that she and Trent would be sharing such newlywed bliss. Laughing and kissing, and touching at every opportunity.

Even…someday…decorating a nursery of their own.

The dream had exploded eleven years ago. She'd swept it into the corners of her mind. It shocked her yesterday to find that the broken shards still retained the power to slash and tear her heart.

By the time he came home that night, she was already in bed.

Like a fool, she lay awake for hours, thinking he might come up to talk to her, to try to explain Missy's call. Or, perhaps, to insist on another…whatever you could call that episode in the cellar.

Sometime during the long hours of last night, waiting for the knock that never came, she had a disturbing revelation. He didn't need to come to her again because, for him, the cellar encounter hadn't been about sex. It hadn't been about passion, or desire, or even leftover yearning from the old days.

It had been about power. She thought about how he had prevented her from touching him. Of course. It made sense now. He hadn't needed any sexual release. All he had needed was to demonstrate that he was in control. That she was a puppet, and he held the strings.

So no. She didn't want him around all day, didn't want him pitching in, as if he was just another one of her friends. She was comfortable with her anger, and she intended to hang on to it. This ricocheting around between emotions—fury, desire, hope and back to fury—was exhausting.

Zander hitched his jeans, clearly irritated by her silence. "What's the problem? We haven't hired anyone to run those acres yet. If Trent takes over, we can open them today."

Practicality warred with emotion. She couldn't deny it would be a help.

Other growers made lots of money with pick-your-own acres, but Everly had never offered the feature before. Her grandfather had thought it would cheapen the orchard's name.

Susannah couldn't see how it could cheapen their name any more than covering half the county in the stink of Everly peaches rotting on the pallets. So she'd decided to try it with a few acres of Gold Prince, one of the few early-ripening semiclings that actually sold well for anything other than canning.

"All right." She tried not to sound ungracious. Zander was doing everything he could to help unload the peaches. At least the pick-your-own acres were on the other side of the property. "Do you think his stitches are healed enough? He'll be up and down ladders all day, helping people."

Zander snorted. "He's fine."

"Did you check the new ladders?"

Immediately after Trent's fall, she'd replaced all the

old ones on the property—about half of everything they owned. The expense of the new ones pinched, but she couldn't risk letting someone else get hurt. Trent might laugh off stitches in his usual macho way, but the next tumble might leave someone truly injured.

"Checked 'em all. Old and new. They're as safe as aces." Zander shook his head. "I don't know what the heck happened to Trent's ladder. I had used that same one just the day before to get to the garage shingles. I didn't break the step, and I'm about fifty pounds heavier than Trent."

"I know. It seems so strange that—"

"Why look!" Zander gestured broadly. "Isn't that your husband over there?"

She looked, and sure enough, Trent was standing by the barn. He leaned against one of the first peach trees, his long torso and narrow hips looking ridiculously sexy, considering he was wearing just jeans and a T-shirt.

He was talking on a cell phone. To Missy Snowdon, no doubt.

She turned to Zander. "I'm sure he's here to talk to you. I'll start briefing the workers."

"No. I'll handle them," Zander said flatly. "You go talk to Trent."

It wasn't something she liked to do, but occasionally Susannah had to remind Zander exactly what was—and wasn't—listed on his job description. Nowhere, she was quite sure, did it include the words "marriage counselor" or "matchmaker."

"Zander."

Her foreman blinked innocently, and she realized just in time that one of the new workers was watching. She sweetened her voice, remembering that a rumor could race through this orchard faster than San Jose scale. "You decided how the pick-your-own acres should be handled, Zander. I expect you to deal with it."

Zander tilted his hat, obviously recognizing the tone that brooked no opposition. She knew that under the wide, shading brim, his eyes would be narrowed in frustration.

Too bad. As he took off, lumbering across the orchard, she looked at Trent, wondering why he'd come. Did he really want to help? Maybe so. She should go over there and thank him for it. After all, the whole purpose of their marriage was to save this peach orchard.

God knows, it wasn't a "real" marriage, for the purpose of love and togetherness. Nothing had brought that home to her more than being together yesterday at Chase's ranch. Two sets of newlyweds, and yet what a difference! It had been all she could do to fight off the bitter pangs of envy she'd felt toward Josie.

That could have been Susannah. It should have been.

Except the man Susannah had been fool enough to want to marry hadn't ever learned the meaning of the word *faithful*.

Only thirty yards away, Trent chatted easily into the phone, his gaze directly on Susannah, watching her watch him. He didn't seem a bit self-conscious. But then, nothing bothered Trent, did it? He was always so stylishly nonchalant, with his devil-black hair and angel-blue eyes. Susannah could already see several of her female friends staring at him—rich, manicured women who were here only to support a friend in need…and, perhaps, to ogle the friend's handsome new husband.

Trent didn't appear to notice them. Without once dropping his gaze from Susannah's, he flipped the cell phone shut and, slipping it into the back pocket of his sinfully sexy jeans, he tossed her a slow wink.

Something deep in her belly pumped heat. As he undoubtedly knew it would.

Bastard, she thought. She turned away. No one needed to worry about Trent's leg. No doubt Missy Snowdon—or whoever had been on the other end of that cell phone—couldn't wait to get her hands on it.

And on the rest of Susannah's husband, too.

BECAUSE TRENT KNEW that Susannah hadn't advertised the pick-your-own acres yet, he had expected to spend a relatively dull morning. He'd even brought his laptop. He thought he might design some flyers to distribute around town, e-mail an ad to the local paper, maybe even update the Everly Web site, all in hopes of drumming up business for the rest of the week.

But apparently he'd underestimated the reputation Everly peaches carried in this town. Word must have spread like chickweed, because by 9:00 a.m. at least a dozen people had arrived, eager to hand him money for the right to pluck their own tree-ripe fruit.

Once the lines of cars were visible from the road, they attracted more people, like honeysuckle drawing hummingbirds. At ten, Trent called the Double C and asked Chase if he had any workers to spare.

It was easy to distinguish the locals, who knew how to pick and had brought their own plastic dishpans, water bottles, sunscreen and well-worn sneakers, from the tourists, who arrived overdressed and eager, bringing nothing but cash and a ton of questions.

"How can I tell if it's ripe?" "What are those little dented places?" "If I want to make ice cream, how many peaches do I need?"

Luckily, Trent remembered the answers. He'd worked alongside Susannah in these orchards every summer from the time they were fourteen, when they were deemed old enough to be useful, right up until Paul died.

Peaches, in fact, had been his entrée into her world. Science teachers like Trent's dad didn't make a lot of money, so when Everly Orchards had advertised for summer workers, Alan Maxwell had applied. On his dad's first day, nine-year-old Trent had ridden his bike over to Everly to bring him lunch. On the way back he passed Susannah, who had been given the chore of minding one of the smaller roadside stands.

"You're standing right next to poison ivy, you know," he'd said, pausing beside the stand, his feet planted wide to balance his bike. Why he'd thought that would be an effective opening line was a mystery to him now. "That plant with the greenish flowers. That's climbing poison ivy."

She had stared down. "It doesn't look like it. It looks like strawberries."

He cringed to remember how he'd launched into a

know-it-all lecture about the different kinds of poison ivy, its effects on humans and animals, and characteristics of urushiols. He must have sounded like a head case, but she'd actually looked interested.

And then, out of nowhere, in a defensive rush, he had blurted out that his dad was one of her dad's summer pickers.

He'd fully expected her pretty little nose to twitch with an heiress's instinctive disdain for the working class. But she had surprised him by sighing enviously. "My dad won't let me do that yet," she'd said. "Not till I'm fourteen."

He'd rested his bike against the wooden wall of the rough-hewn stand and bought a peach with his last dime, just so that he wouldn't have to leave. And then he got lucky. A couple of snotty jerks from Blanco Falls, one of the biggest ranches in the county, had come sauntering by and, purely for the fun of tormenting a pretty girl, had stolen a handful of peaches.

Later, Trent couldn't really remember why he'd done it—whether it was to impress her, or merely because the injustice offended his idealistic young psyche—but he took off after them and demanded they give the peaches back.

They'd refused. One of them had punched Trent in the shoulder, and the other called Susannah a dirty word. Before he knew it, Trent had the bigger, meaner boy on the ground and was opening a stream of blood from the kid's nose.

The peaches had been ruined, of course, and the boys had told their parents, who'd called Trent's father, and

Trent had been grounded for a month. But every day of that month, Susannah had ridden her bike the three miles from Everly to the Maxwell shotgun cottage on the edge of town and left him a fresh peach on the front porch.

When they'd started school in the fall, without a word of explanation, Susannah had sat beside him at lunch. For an awkward ten minutes, no one had joined them. And then Chase Clayton and Paul Archer, two of the richest kids in the school, had dumped their trays on the table.

"The Blanco boys suck," Chase had said, sitting down with a smile. From that moment on, miraculously, Trent had been one of them.

He took a deep breath now, inhaling the scent of sweet peaches, which, he knew, would always remind him of Susannah. Then he put the memories back in the closet. He was here to help her save these orchards, and he'd better get busy doing it.

Over in the second row of trees, an hourglass-shaped trophy wife with a diamond ring the size of a peach pit stood on a ladder, yanking off fruit and dropping it into her basket. Making every mistake in the book.

When she got home and unpacked a bushel of bruised peaches, naturally she'd blame the orchard, not herself. And goodbye great reputation.

Trent made his way over to her ladder. Her perfume overpowered the smell of the peaches, which wasn't easy to do.

"Hey," he called casually. "Remember, you want to try to use the sides of your fingers. Not the tips."

The woman looked down at him, scanning his body

from forehead to toe. When her gaze came back up, she smiled. He knew that smile well, the one that said she was either divorced or wished she were.

"Really? Why is that?"

"A peach bruises easily. With the tips of your fingers, it's easy to exert too much pressure."

"Sounds tricky." She caught her lower lip between her teeth and smiled even more deeply. "I'm Becky. Why don't you come up and show me?"

She was gorgeous, he had to admit that. And he knew exactly how seductive he could make these peaches sound. How the tender, velvety-furred flesh required just the right touch. How the soft fruit inside, still warm from the sun, would release juices that would run down your chin.

How enduring a dry spell sometimes intensified their sweetness. How the peach separated easily from the tree when it was ripe enough, and practically fell into your hands.

As he'd realized more than once, he was no saint. He actually gave it a half second's thought. He knew a ripe woman as well as he knew a ripe peach, and this one would be easy to harvest. And, frankly, this celibacy thing was getting a bit rough.

But he had about a hundred powerful reasons to say no—a list that started with the diamond ring on Becky's finger and ended with the one on Susannah's.

"It's no big deal," he said, pretending he hadn't noticed the come-on. "You'll get the hang of it. Place the peaches gently in your basket, and try not to heap them more than about fourteen inches deep. The fruit on the bottom can't take the pressure."

Becky looked surprised, as if her invitations weren't often refused. "Okay," she said. "But are you sure—"

"Maxwell!"

Trent turned in the direction of the voice, glad of any excuse to move away from the woman's predatory gaze. But his relief was short-lived. The man marching across the orchard was Richard Doyle, old man Everly's lawyer. He wore a suit, so he wasn't here for a peach fix.

"Excuse me," Trent said to the woman on the ladder. "Business."

He reached Doyle just as the lawyer cleared the checkout table, where Richie, one of the younger ranch hands from the Double C, was busy selling water, snacks and picking containers next to the woman from Everly who was weighing and packaging the peaches.

Doyle stopped. "I need to talk to you, Maxwell."

Trent didn't know the man all that well, but he assumed that the gruff, bass-note tone wasn't his natural voice. And surely the lawyer didn't walk around with that X-shaped groove between his eyebrows. He was obviously in a major snit.

"Okay." Trent shrugged. "Here I am. Talk."

The lawyer cast a dark glance toward the table. "I think you might prefer to have this conversation in private."

Damn, this guy had pompous down pat. He couldn't be more than thirty-five, but he acted sixty. Trent tilted his head and smiled, mostly because he knew it would infuriate the other man.

"Quite honestly, I'd rather not have this conversation

at all." He raised one eyebrow. "But I'm guessing that's not an option?"

Doyle's jaw tightened. "You're damn right it's not."

"Okay, then. As I said, I'm here. But I won't be forever. Talk."

"Have it your way." Doyle took a breath and hitched his slacks. "I came because Susannah wanted me to give you some papers. But first I'd like to give you a chance to explain yourself."

Trent chuckled. "Explain myself? I'm afraid tha* might take more time than I've got. And maybe a couple of psychiatrists."

"For God's sake, Maxwell." Doyle's shoulders stiffened. "I have some pretty damaging information here. Do you insist on turning everything into a joke?"

"On the contrary. I'm constantly in search of something I can take seriously." Trent glanced at the orchard, where another family had arrived, this one with two young boys who would probably destroy everything they touched. "How about if we get to the point? What is this *information* you think you have?"

"Not think. *Know.*" Doyle grimaced. "I've had someone looking into what you were doing during the years you were gone. And I found out some mighty disturbing information about one Virginia Windsor Smith."

"Ginny is hardly a secret," Trent said. "She's a fairly prominent almond grower out in California."

"She's more than that. She's a beautiful, rich woman. A very innocent, trusting sort of woman. And she's your ex-wife."

"Also not a secret. If you're thinking this will shock

Susannah, think again. She knows I've been married before, and she doesn't care. She probably appreciates that someone else saddle broke me for her."

That might have been a step too far. But Trent's temper was rising, which always made him more sarcastic. Why the hell had this bastard been out in California harassing Ginny?

"I hope your detective didn't charge you much," he added pleasantly. "Sounds as if he missed the other six ex-wives, the ones I keep locked up in the basement."

"Maybe. But he didn't miss the five hundred acres of prime California agricultural land you weaseled out of her."

Trent raised his eyebrows. "Ginny is one of the most successful almond farmers in California. I'd like to meet the man who could weasel anything out of her."

Doyle put his hands in his pockets, as if he was afraid he might succumb to the urge to punch Trent in the face.

Trent was working through a similar impulse. Everything about this man irritated him. Doyle was probably considered good-looking by most female standards, with his chiseled features and spiky, modish blond hair, but Trent thought he looked like a bird still wet from the egg.

"You signed a prenup with Virginia Windsor Smith, just like you did with Susannah." Doyle tightened his eyes. "I'm looking for proof, and when I get it I'm going to take it to Susannah. I wonder if she will think it's so funny when she hears you somehow made your ex-wife pay you to go away."

"You know, for a lawyer, that's pretty sloppy logic."

Trent smiled. "Look it up. I'm pretty sure you'll find that correlation does not imply causation."

"You smug son of a—" Doyle stopped himself, but the skin around his nostrils was pure white. "I'm not just a lawyer, Maxwell. I'm also a rancher's son, and we learn early around here that if your boots stink, you've stepped in shit. And everything you touch ends up stinking. That's all the logic I need to know."

"Charmingly folksy," Trent said. "But you said you had some papers for me?"

With stiff movements. the lawyer reached into his inside breast pocket and pulled out an envelope. "I want to go on record with you, as I did with Susannah, as objecting to this proposal. I think it's the worst possible reaction to whatever emotional blackmail you're trying. It's beneath her."

"May I see?"

Doyle thrust out the envelope, as if he had to force himself to relinquish it. Trent opened it and scanned it quickly. The legalese was dense and idiotic, but it was essentially the deal Susannah had offered him the other day. If he didn't run around having sex with his millions of trashy girlfriends during the year he was married to St. Susannah, she'd pay him $120,000.

Ten grand for every month of celibacy, just as she'd suggested. She must really think Trent had trouble keeping his pants on. He wondered whether it was Missy Snowdon's call the other day that had prompted her to make the offer official.

Or perhaps she just enjoyed insulting him.

"Interesting," he said, keeping his face relaxed, though

he felt his temper teetering dangerously on the edge of explosion. "Doesn't work out to be much, figured as an hourly wage. But I'll have my lawyer look at it and get back to you."

Doyle narrowed his eyes. "Would you really consider signing such a demeaning document? Would you really take that money from her?"

Trent laughed as he slid the envelope into his back pocket. "Who knows? It's not exactly five hundred acres of prime California agricultural land, but it's a nice chunk of change."

CHAPTER EIGHT

EVERY JUNE 5, Susannah sneaked away from the bustle of peach picking and made a solitary trek to Green Fern Pool. There, cool and hidden from the rest of the world, she could whisper happy birthday to Paul Archer in the place he had loved the best.

This year, getting away had been more difficult than ever. It was almost 6 p.m. before she ducked under the arch created by the low branches of two black gum trees, which the Fugitive Four had dubbed "Heaven's Gate," and entered their secret hideaway.

Groaning softly, her arms already aching after only a few days of picking, she lowered herself onto the flat rock they had called the boat launch and gazed out onto the swimming hole.

Sometimes it was crystal blue and green, alive with sunshine, clear enough to see the rainbow-colored rocks scattered across the sandy bottom.

But not today. All afternoon, the sky had been darkening, gathering rain, and the murky water undulated under invisible gusts of the impending storm. Behind the pale oval reflection of Susannah's face, looming silhouettes of ancient trees shifted ominously.

God, she was tired. The boat launch rock was wide and flat, and she wished she could just lie down on it and take a nap. She'd slept here a hundred times, curled up on this rock with Trent's arms wrapped around her, listening dreamily to the splash and laughter of Paul and Chase doing cannonballs off the limestone walls.

But today's birthday memorial would have to be short. No time for naps or sentimental reminiscing. No time even to let her aching shoulders relax.

She dug in her pocket for the pebble she'd brought with her. She warmed it inside her palm, blew to transform it into a wishing stone, then tossed it out into the center of the pool.

Chase had started this tradition, and through the years they'd come here to wish for all the dumb stuff typical teenagers desired. For cool cars and hot clothes, for Chase to get good SAT scores and for Paul to pitch a no-hitter. For easy Spanish tests, and no zits on prom night.

And then there had been the day—they'd been seventeen that summer—when Trent had stood on the edge of the rock and grinned evilly at Susannah. "Next time we have a pool party, I wish Missy Snowdon's breasts would bust right out of her bikini," he'd cried to the water gods.

Susannah, who thought he was just being an idiot, had pushed him into the pool, jeans and sneakers and all. And everyone had laughed.

"Happy birthday, Paul," she whispered as the pebble sank. And then, as she did every year, she added, "I wish you were here."

It was inevitable, at this moment, that she would live it all again.

It had been stupid from the start, the kind of immature scheme only a spoiled, heartbroken teenager could devise.

The five of them, the Fugitive Four and Chase's new, obnoxious wife—had plans to go drinking at a hokey little hoedown bar on the outskirts of Eastcreek that night.

Two nights after she had watched Trent and Missy make love in the rain.

Her grandfather's guests were still in town, keeping her busy, so Trent didn't know he'd been caught, not yet. She didn't want him to know, because she had a plan.

She dressed carefully that night. She wanted to look fantastic. She wanted Trent panting for her. And then she was going to ignore him. She was going to flirt and dance with Paul. Then, when Trent dared to object, she was going to hit him with what she knew.

At first, it had seemed the plan would work. While Susannah and Paul slow-danced to Tammy Wynette, Trent sat in the corner, glowering, getting angrier by the minute. Chase's wife, Lila, who was a few years older than the Fugitive Four and supplying the drinks for the whole table, had found it all hilarious. She'd kept the liquor flowing freely, just to see what would happen.

And then, as if lightning had reached into the tacky bar, with its hay on the floor and kerosene lanterns for mood lighting, everything went horribly, tragically wrong.

Out of nowhere, Paul and Trent began to fight, and within three seconds, long before even a sober person could react, the hay was on fire. And so was Paul.

Trent fell on him, rolling Paul away as if he could put out the flames with only his body—although someone dragged him off before he, too, could become engulfed in the fire. Chase was more sensible, and tore off his shirt and jacket, and tried to smother the flames. A hard-eyed waitress found a bucket of water and tossed it onto the burning, writhing figure that Susannah knew was Paul.

Eventually something worked, but not before Paul had been burned beyond recognition. Beyond hope.

In her memory, the moment was always eerily silent, as if the screams that filled the bar that night had left her deaf. Her screams, and Paul's, and the other guests', who were stampeding for the door.

"I'm sorry, Paul," she whispered now, as she did every year. And then, sometimes, after the pebble's ripples died away, she cried a little. It was the only place she could let herself fall apart.

But today she was simply too tired for tears. She couldn't feel much of anything, except the ache in her arms.

Maybe it was time to give up this pointless pilgrimage. Paul wasn't here, and he never would be, not even if she filled Green Fern Pool to the brim with pebbles.

She hoisted herself to her feet, climbed back up the sandy track that led to the real world, and made her way to her car. She cast a worried look at the sky, which was more threatening than ever. She hoped she hadn't lost her last hour of picking time.

As she headed back to Everly, she was speeding a little, so she almost didn't see the other car pulled off by the side of the road, maybe a quarter of a mile from the head of the Green Fern trail.

Few people took this small side road. Could someone else have been making a pilgrimage, too?

She slowed, curious. She'd never seen anyone else at the pool on Paul's birthday. The anniversary of his death was coming up soon, only a little more than three weeks away. That, not the birthday, seemed to be the occasion Mr. and Mrs. Archer annually honored by visiting the cemetery, separately leaving large bouquets of flowers.

But as she drew closer, she recognized Peggy Archer's car. Peggy had pulled it off onto the shoulder, and it was easy to see why. The back right tire was completely flat, and the car tilted helplessly toward the wounded side.

Peggy herself sat crossways on the driver's seat, her legs out the door, her head in her hands. Her hair was a mess, and her face was red, as if she'd been in the muggy heat a long time.

Susannah wasn't sure what to do. Of all the people in the world who might stop to play Good Samaritan, Susannah would be Peggy's last choice. Especially today.

But she couldn't just drive by as if she didn't see her. Susannah knew how to change a tire, of course, and she could have Peggy back on the road in minutes.

So she eased over, joining Peggy's car on the right of way, and set her hazard lights to flash. Even with little traffic, the weather was gloomy enough to make it risky, here on the curve of the road.

"Hello, Mrs. Archer," she said politely as she walked up to the disabled car. "Looks as if you've had some trouble. If you've got a spare, I would be happy to put it on for you."

Peggy lifted her head, and Susannah realized that she'd been crying. It stopped her in her tracks, as shocking as if the woman had turned out to be naked.

Peggy wasn't a weeper. For six months, Susannah had come every day to Paul's hospital bed, where Peggy had sat, staring blank-eyed at the ruins of her son. Not once in all those months had Peggy spoken a word to Susannah.

And never once had Susannah seen her shed a tear.

"Are you all right, Mrs. Archer? I have some water in the car…"

Peggy struggled to her feet, clearly favoring her left leg. Holding on to the car door with one hand, she wiped briskly under her eyes with the other.

"I'm fine. The auto club is coming." She looked at her watch. "They should have been here half an hour ago."

She tried to take a step, but the pain was evident on her face. "I would change it myself. It's just that my hip… getting down like that…" She touched her left leg. "I took a second pain pill, hoping it would help—"

"What is it?" Instinctively, Susannah reached out. "Are you hurt?"

Peggy recoiled, as if Susannah were a snake striking. "I'm fine." She took a jagged breath. "I mean, it's just arthritis."

Just arthritis? Susannah saw sweat breaking out on

the older woman's brow and upper lip. Simply standing here like this had flooded her with pain.

"Please, Mrs. Archer. Why don't you sit in my car while I change the tire? The keys are in the ignition. Turn the air on and get comfortable. It'll only take a few minutes."

Peggy shut her eyes, and the veins at her temples pulsed under the sweat-shining skin. "Perhaps I should," she said, her shoulders sagging as if she'd just lost some kind of battle. She reached into the car and pulled out an aluminum cane. "The pill can leave me a little dizzy."

After that flinch a minute ago, Susannah knew better than to put her arm under Peggy's elbow, but it was difficult to watch the woman limp away. Peggy hung on to her own car's bulk as long as she could and then lurched the rest of the way, supported only by the cane.

When had this happened to her? This feisty, fabulous woman used to run the domestic side of the ten-thousand-acre Bull's Eye ranch like clockwork, while still finding time to chair the PTA, the Little League and the Community Coordinating Council. And she always had a few minutes left over to make mouthwatering blueberry muffins to sustain the Fugitive Four when they got the urge to wander.

Now she couldn't walk ten steps. A muffled cry escaped Peggy's tight lips as she lowered herself onto Susannah's driver's seat. The cane clattered to the ground.

Susannah moved to recover it.

"No. Thank you," Peggy said stiffly. "I think we should hurry. It's going to rain."

"Of course. You're right."

Susannah got busy. She worked as fast as she could, aware of the other woman's gaze boring into her back. She wondered if she should try to make small talk, but couldn't think of anything that Peggy would want to hear.

She wondered again what Peggy was doing here. She knew that she had moved to Darlonsville immediately after her divorce—maybe nine years ago now. The woman seemed to avoid Eastcreek, and why shouldn't she? Here, everything would remind her of Paul.

As far as Susannah knew, Peggy came into town only once a year…to visit Paul's grave on the anniversary of his death. Even if she'd decided to mark his birthday, she wouldn't do it here, at Green Fern Pool.

The Fugitive Four had always vowed that, when they died, they wanted to be cremated and scattered over Green Fern Pool. Chase had been the only one brave enough, or innocent enough, to mention Paul's wish to Peggy and Harrison Archer.

According to Chase, Peggy's reaction had been kind of crazy. Cremate her beautiful son? Scatter his ashes in the place he'd shared with his *friends?* Chase had replicated the sarcastic emphasis on "friends".

Never. Chase had told them her voice was so cold, so thick with hatred, that it scared the hell out of him. When they killed her son, they lost their right to him.

Paul belonged to her now.

Though the hot afternoon was humid, the pavement beside the car steaming with every stray raindrop, Susannah felt a shiver zip up her back.

She turned her head, driven by a sudden need to be sure Peggy was still sitting in the car.

She was. She was massaging her left leg, running her thumbs hard along the muscle, from hip to knee and back again. Her face was tight, lined with pain.

Susannah's hands stilled on the lug wrench. How unfair. After all Peggy had already endured...

There should be some kind of limit on suffering.

"I'm sorry your leg is giving you so much trouble. Is there anything they can do to help?"

Peggy looked up. Her eyes were red, and a little glazed, as if the pills might have kicked in a bit too much, though they obviously hadn't touched the pain.

"It's not always this bad," Peggy said in an oddly dreamy voice. Her thumbs kept tracing her thigh muscle, though she fixed her slightly off-kilter gaze directly on Susannah. The effect was unsettling, as if her body and her mind weren't quite in sync.

"It's my own fault. I exacerbated it," Peggy went on in that trancelike way. "I walked too far, and I paid the price."

Susannah returned to attaching the lug nuts, though her fingers were clumsy on the wrench, and the silver bullet-like fasteners kept dropping onto the ground and skittering away.

What did Peggy mean? Where had she walked? There was almost nothing out here, nothing but Green Fern Pool.

"Were you...where did you go?"

For an uncomfortable second, silence hung in the air. In the distance, thunder growled, and a drop of rain landed on Susannah's cheek. In her peripheral vision she could still see Peggy kneading her aching leg.

Finally the woman made a noise that sounded like a low laugh. "You know where I went. I went to the pool."

Susannah turned again. "To Green Fern Pool?"

Peggy nodded, still stroking rhythmically, still staring at Susannah without blinking.

"Why?"

Slowly, Peggy smiled. "I was watching you."

TRENT HAD WAITED three days, carrying around the two pieces of the contract, which he had torn in half as soon as Doyle left the orchard. He had hoped that, if he waited long enough, his anger would cool.

Not that he had much chance to talk to Susannah privately anyhow. She never seemed to be alone these days.

She worked the orchard from dawn to dusk, and at night she recruited Chase and Josie, and her friend Nell Bollinger, and even some of the part-time pickers, to help her at the house.

It was like a big, happy commune, everyone working together in the spacious Everly kitchen, canning and freezing and cooking and pickling.

Making sure not one slice of the unsold peaches went to waste.

Trent wasn't invited, which was fine with him. He handled the pick-your-own fields all day, and at night he went to the Double C, to catch up on his real job. By the time he dragged his ass back to Everly, Susannah was sound asleep, and he was too damned tired to care.

But on the third night, Trent didn't close down the pick-your-own acres until long after twilight. After leaving the cash for deposit with Zander and discussing tomorrow's schedule, he wasn't in the mood to start over at the Double C.

He rolled into Everly's driveway about ten o'clock, at least two hours earlier than usual. As he let himself in the front door, he was surprised to find the house completely quiet. He'd expected to hear the usual cacophony of pots bubbling, bottles clattering, blenders whining.

But the first floor was dark, except for one desk lamp on the landing, which she must have left on so that he wouldn't kill himself on the stairs.

He laughed a little, the sound oddly unpleasant in the cool stillness of the shadowy foyer. Maybe he really should ask Doyle what the will said about her inheritance if she suddenly became a widow. Did she have to start the year over with another sucker, or did she immediately acquire all the power without having to endure twelve months of marriage?

The sight of him tumbling down those stairs to his death might be her most delicious secret fantasy.

He knew how unfair that was, but he didn't much care.

Boy, was he in a crummy mood or what?

Damn it, though, Doyle had really pissed him off, with his accusations and his "contracts" that were little more than blackmail.

And, frankly, so did everything else about this "marriage." What had made him think he could handle this? What kind of masochist signed up to spend every night ten yards away from the woman he wanted so bad it was like starving?

He was halfway up the stairs when he heard the

distant whistle of water. Everly's old pipes, narrowed by decades of rust, always complained whenever anyone took a shower.

It had been useful, back when they were teenagers. The sound of the pipes singing, which signaled her grandfather's shower, had been the background music for some pretty hot sessions on the library sofa.

Damn it. He stopped on the landing, feeling his body growing hard just remembering. He hadn't seen her naked in more than ten years, but he knew how she would look right now, as she stepped into the shower.

Her breasts would have a copper glow above the shirt line in spite of the repeated latherings of sunscreen, but the rest of her, the secret parts of her, would be white and smooth.

Her breasts would be high, small but full. Her legs would be long, her belly flat. Her fingers slim and nimble...

He shut his eyes, trying to fight it. But his heart raced, and the throb under his jeans was unendurable. He moved quickly, pulling his shirt over his head as he went.

As he passed through her bedroom, he dropped the pieces of Doyle's contract onto her bed. If she wondered later what had driven him to act so impulsively, this would be her answer.

How many times would he have to explain that he didn't want her money? He wanted only what he'd been promised. A real marriage that didn't consist of three hundred and sixty-five nights of torture.

His belt slapped onto the dresser. His jeans and shoes came off at the bathroom threshold.

He didn't knock, didn't ask for permission he knew he wouldn't receive. She'd given her permission when she made her original deal with him, and again when she agreed in the wine cellar that she had an obligation to honor it.

He simply opened the shower door and stepped in.

With a small cry, she turned, the bar of soap falling from her hands and thudding at her feet. Her face paled with absolute terror.

Damn it. He'd been ready for fury, but he hadn't meant to frighten her. He felt strangely ashamed. As always, the real, flesh-and-blood Susannah, the fragile, brave-hearted beauty he'd loved since he was ten, unsettled him.

She was so different from the brittle devil woman of his imagination.

"It's okay," he said, instantly contrite. He scooped her soapy body into his arms. "It's just me, Sue. It's just me."

Almost as soon as he spoke, he realized she might have known it was him. Her fear might well be of Trent himself, not some stranger who might have broken into the house.

This was insane. Maybe she had been right about him all along. Maybe he was just a selfish bastard.

He should leave her alone.

But once he had touched her, it was too late.

She hadn't pulled away, and he didn't intend to wait for her to reconsider.

"Trent," she said, her voice shaking.

Before she could say another word, he kissed her hard on the lips, tasting water and soap and heat and peaches.

Oh, he was lost. The skin of her gracefully muscled back was slick under his hands. Without thinking, he stroked up to her shoulders, and then down to her ass, which was so tight and perfect that he groaned as he cupped it in his hungry palms.

Their lips still locked, he tilted her closer, against the erection that was impossibly rigid and full, and slid easily into the soapy, peach-fuzz warmth between her legs. Her breasts pressed against his chest, and the warm jets of the shower spilled onto his face.

He tried to catch his breath, and couldn't.

It really was like the first time all over again, as if his body were new to him and not yet under his control. He thought he might come right that minute, just from the pebbled thrust of her nipples against his skin, and the secret, wet warmth of her mouth. Just from the way her silky thighs and her soft pubic hair felt against his penis.

He seemed to be made of a hundred million nerves, every one on fire. The water was so hot, and the shower was thick with steam, enveloping the two of them in a sensual cocoon.

He felt oddly helpless, unable to think clearly, unable to feel anything except the burning torture between his legs.

Without warning, she broke off the kiss. She looked at him for one long second, and then she reached down and took the length of him into her palm.

He cried out, the fire screaming through him as he swelled even more, beyond what any man could bear.

"No," he said. "Wait."

She didn't wait. Her hand was firm, knowing and deliberate. She moved back and forth, and he throbbed and flamed, and called out again. He stepped back, but his shoulders met the shower wall, and there was no escape.

He couldn't stand it. He tried to remember what he should do...there was something he should do for her....

But he couldn't think. He wasn't a man anymore. He was just a piece of fiery flesh, helpless in her hands. When she knelt down and pulled him into her mouth, he groaned at the relief. He grabbed her wet head between his palms for balance.

"Susannah," he cried and the orgasm was almost instantaneous. He was no more able to prevent the beautiful explosion, the shudders of agonizing pleasure, the pulses of white joy, than he could have if he were already dead.

She didn't rush it. It seemed to last forever, but when it finally ended, when the last, drained throb had died away, she stood and moved from him without speaking.

Without even looking at him.

She turned her face to the shower, and opened her mouth, so that the warm water would wash all traces of him away. She rinsed the rest of her body, sluicing off the lingering white trails of soap.

Then she put her hand around the shower door and plucked a towel from the rack.

"And now," she said as she covered herself, "you know how it feels."

CHAPTER NINE

THE DAY BEFORE the annual peach party, Susannah had set her alarm for quarter to dawn.

She had to superclean the house today, though she was dreading it like torture. Everything, from the attic to the basement, was a mess. She hadn't had a spare minute in the past three weeks, and she couldn't bear to think about what all that cooking had done to the kitchen....

"Be quiet." She fumbled for the snooze bar and hit it for the third time. "I can't face it yet."

She tried to pull the pillow over her head, but the muscles in her arms screamed that the pillow was made of lead and couldn't be moved. She collapsed with a groan. How were those burned-out arms going to sweep and vacuum, polish and wax?

She still had thirty-six hours till the party. Maybe, if she started phoning people right now...

But she knew she couldn't bring herself to call it off.

Thirty years ago, on the day Susannah was born, her grandfather had christened the tradition of the annual Everly peach party. He'd had a good business head back then, and he'd seen the advantage of combining a touching family celebration with a little public relations.

She often wondered whether he would have bothered if her mother hadn't gone into labor at a lucky time, during that peaceful moment between the Harvesters and the Red Globes, when the orchards seemed to pause and take a breath.

He already had all those workers on the payroll, and no peaches to pick. They might as well be doing something.

Since then, the tradition had never skipped a year. He'd even passed up the chance to plant Lorings, which would have ripened during the hiatus.

It was one of the few things they both loved, and they kept the ceremony intact as a way of keeping the family together. When her parents died, he hosted it in their honor. When he was addled with dementia, Susannah hosted it in his.

Of course, back in her grandfather's day, three maids had scoured the house, top to bottom, washing crystal, polishing silver and rubbing wood till it gleamed. Two chefs had bustled about the kitchen, creating the wonders to wow the guests and secure the reputation of Everly peaches for another year to come.

Even last year, she'd had one maid left in the house. And Nikki, though she was a sullen worker at best. This time, it was just Susannah, and any friends softhearted enough to take pity on her.

Chase and Josie had been lifesavers this past week, helping her whip up pies and ice cream and jams and salsas, using the recipes in the burn center's new cookbook, which they'd give to the guests tomorrow night.

She forced herself to sit up, though the small of her back protested.

"Damn it." She slid her legs slowly over the side of the bed, ignoring the ribbon of pain along the front of her thighs. Even her toes hurt. That's what nearly a month of dawn-to-dusk peach picking could do.

Suddenly, something started to roar just outside her bedroom door.

She eased herself to a standing position. The roar sounded suspiciously like a vacuum cleaner, but frankly it didn't matter what was out there. A rabid Minotaur could be racing down the hallway, planning to gobble her for breakfast, and she couldn't move any faster. It took ten minutes minimum to loosen up these abused muscles.

She tugged her T-shirt, hoping it covered her bottom, limped across the room and opened her door.

A beautiful young blonde in skintight blue jeans stood at the end of the hall, right in front of Susannah's grandfather's room. Correction. Trent's room now. The blonde was, indeed, wielding a very large vacuum cleaner.

When she saw Susannah, she reached down and flipped the switch. The roar died away.

"I'm sorry," the blonde said. "I hope I didn't wake you up."

Susannah looked down the hall, where another young woman was squatting, dusting the complicated carved legs of the half-moon hall table. Susannah wondered whether she might still be asleep and having a lovely dream.

The blonde fiddled with the vacuum's cord, trying to free it from a chair leg. "They said it was okay to start vacuuming once it turned seven o'clock."

Susannah blinked. "Who is 'they'?"

The blonde's finger played over the vacuum's *on* switch, itching to get going. "I don't know. You know. Home-Maid Harmony? We work for them."

She stared at Susannah, clearly wondering whether she might be mentally deficient. "You know? The people you hired?"

"But I didn't—"

"No, that's okay." Trent appeared at the head of the stairs. He smiled at the annoyed blonde, and of course her annoyance melted away like sugar in the rain. "I did."

Susannah felt suddenly awkward, with her raggedy T-shirt, bare legs and feet, an unmistakable absence of underclothes and a serious case of bedhead.

She tugged at her T-shirt again. "You hired a cleaning company?"

He nodded. "I thought you could use some help."

"Thanks, but I'm fine. Really."

Both maids were watching curiously. As if they were the lead actors in a play, Trent came over and put his knuckle under her chin. The loving husband.

Oh, why hadn't she anticipated that this marriage would require so much *pretense?*

She had avoided him for nearly three weeks now, since the episode in the shower. Big-time avoidance. The back-out-of-the-drive-if-you-see-his-car kind of avoidance.

Not easy, given how closely they worked and lived together. It had been like one of those logic puzzles. You have a lamb, a wolf and some lettuce, and you have to transport them across the river without ever letting the wolf be alone with the lamb, or the lamb be alone with the lettuce.

After she'd left him in the shower that night, she'd found the contract offering him $120,000, neatly ripped in half, scattered on the middle of her bed.

She could add two and two as well as anyone. Coupled with the brazen assertion of his marital rights that followed, that destroyed document was a message. An echo, really, of the things he'd already said. He didn't want her money, but he did want her body. He felt entitled to take it whenever he chose.

At first she'd felt pleased with herself, as if, by controlling the experience, she'd won. Given him a taste of his own medicine. Taught him a lesson.

But when she saw him out in the orchard the next day, he hadn't looked one bit chastened. He'd smiled with his usual charm and perhaps even an extra dash of roguish amusement.

Of course. What a fool she was. What had she expected? Men didn't exactly blush and fluster because a naked woman decided to service them free of charge. It was undoubtedly every red-blooded man's favorite fantasy.

And the worst thing was that, just as had happened after the episode in the cellar, *she* thought about it all the time. *All the time.* She had never been so turned on in her life. She buzzed with sexual awareness. She was actually afraid that, if he came too close, he would be able to hear the sizzle. To smell the hunger.

That was why she worked so hard at avoiding him. And she actually had a strange feeling that he was cooperating. It was almost as if he realized that she'd been unnerved by what she'd done and wanted to give her some space.

He stayed out in the orchard later, spent longer hours at the Double C afterward. She might have suspected that he was seeing Missy Snowdon, except that he didn't have time. She heard regularly from both Zander and Chase, and every single hour of Trent's day and night was accounted for.

"The party's tomorrow," he said. "You didn't think I was going to let you do all this alone, did you?"

Yes, that was exactly what she'd thought, but she managed not to say so.

"Thank you, really. But it's not necessary." She backed up slightly, so that his hand lost contact with her chin. "I can handle it."

The blonde scowled hard, as if she saw her paycheck slipping away. "Look, all six of us have already scheduled the day—"

Susannah gasped. "Six of you?"

Trent raised his eyebrows. "Apparently you haven't seen the kitchen lately. Six is the bare minimum, I'd say."

She hesitated, knowing he was right. But she didn't have the money, and she didn't want him spending his money, either. Not on her.

"Trent—"

"Excuse us," he said politely to the maids. Then, without asking permission, he pressed on the door, widening the opening, grabbed her hand and pulled her into the bedroom. He shut the door behind them.

The drumbeat low in her midsection began to pound lightly. Her lungs tightened. What was he going to do? One whisk of this T-shirt, ten steps to the bed, and they could be…

She lifted her chin and glared at him, warning him not to cross the line.

To her surprise, the expression on his face was gentle. He reached out and tucked a stray hair behind her ear. She ordinarily wore it braided when she slept, but last night she couldn't lift her arms above her head long enough to do the job.

"Don't be childish about it. Let's just say it's my birthday present to you."

"We don't give each other birthday presents."

But she heard how immature and sullen she sounded. And, against her will, she remembered other birthdays, with daisy-crowns and picnics, with CDs and books, with gold lockets and brown kittens and kisses.

"Be practical," he said. "You don't have enough hours left to do it by yourself. Let the maids work here today. I saw your list of errands on the kitchen table. Get dressed, and we'll go run some of them."

We'll run them? *We?*

Something tight inside her chest loosened as she realized the nightmare of today could, with his help, morph into something much nicer. A day without pain and desperation. A day without loneliness.

All she had to do was say yes. Graciously, with a *thank you* attached.

"I—I don't know—"

"Sue, don't be an idiot. We'll be at the grocery store, at the bank. What could possibly happen?"

She felt herself blushing. So he knew what she really feared. She feared that, somewhere in all this chivalric heroism, he might feel that he'd earned the right to touch her. And she feared that, if he did, he might ignite that fire she was trying so hard to keep banked.

"Look, here's how I see it. For the moment, the score between us is tied, one all." He smiled. "So how about we declare a truce? Just until the peach party is over."

He held out his hand. "Come on. We're too exhausted to make war *or* love very effectively right now."

She took a breath and studied him. She could find no hidden meanings in his words. No sardonic gleam behind his blue eyes. No tricks up his crisp white sleeves.

She *would* be a fool to say no. It would have been pointless, anyhow, because the blonde, who obviously wasn't a patient woman, had flicked the switch, and the vacuum had roared back into life.

So instead of answering at all, Susannah merely reached out and shook his warm, strong hand.

And tried, God help her, to ignore how dangerously sexy it felt.

TRENT WAS IMPRESSED. Clearly Susannah had the instincts of a field general. Her chores had been mapped out geographically, her grocery list was arranged to correspond to the contents of each aisle, and, whenever necessary, she called ahead to be certain the people and supplies she needed were readily available.

She even knew how to diplomatically dispatch unexpected social contacts, which might have slowed her down. He marveled as she gave each friend the perfect amount of attention required by courtesy. Three minutes for Nell Bollinger, two for a doctor from the burn center, just thirty seconds for Bucky Sizemore's wife, who everyone knew was a bitch.

Susannah was so clever about it that no one seemed slighted—except perhaps Eli Breslin, whom they passed outside the drugstore. Eli earned only a wave, and the boy gave Trent a nasty glare to show that he knew where the blame should fall.

It could have been worse. Trent glimpsed Missy Snowdon in the wine shop, but he was pretty sure neither woman noticed the other one. Now *that* would have been bad luck.

By three o'clock, when he and Susannah stopped for a quick lunch at an outdoor café, they had accomplished every errand on her daunting list. And they hadn't had a single moment of discord.

Six whole hours of cease-fire. That was a world record, at least in the years since Paul's death.

He wondered how long he could stretch it out.

She collapsed onto the metal chair with a sigh. "I can't believe it," she said. "I didn't expect to have time for a meal today. Or tomorrow, for that matter. I thought I might be able to grab a peach, but that's about it."

He arranged the few packages they carried in the space between their chairs. Most of the supplies had been delivered to Everly, where Zander would sign for them and put them away.

"Frankly, I'd rather starve than eat another peach," Trent said with a laugh. "I want a hamburger the size of a truck."

She picked up the menu. "Me, too. Well, not a hamburger, of course, but something huge and—"

She looked up as a sudden shadow passed over their table. Trent felt his shoulders tighten instinctively as he realized it was Harrison Archer, with his younger red-headed son in tow.

"I'm sorry to interrupt," Harrison said stiffly. He clearly wanted his smile to look normal, but he wasn't having much success. Trent wondered how many words Harrison and Susannah had exchanged in the past ten years. Maybe ten? Twenty?

None?

Even the little boy looked nervous, as if he sensed that this wasn't an ordinary stop for chitchat. Trent smiled at the kid, hoping to make him feel more at ease, but the boy's sober expression didn't change.

"It's all right, Mr. Archer," Susannah said politely. "We haven't ordered yet."

She waited, clearly unsure what came next.

Harrison didn't speak for a couple of seconds. Trent dropped his menu, feeling a primitive need to have his hands free, just in case. Which was ridiculous, since, thanks to the healing arrival of his new family, Harrison seemed to have moved beyond hostility toward either Susannah or Trent years ago.

Still…it felt weird, how the guy had appeared out of nowhere. He wasn't projecting his usual good-old-boy bluster. He looked a little off, with heavy bags under his eyes, as if he hadn't slept in days.

Of course, it was harvesttime on the Bull's Eye ranch, too. With that many acres, the Archers were always harvesting something.

"I wanted to thank you for the invitation to the peach party," Harrison said finally. He put his hand on his son's shoulder. "I know you always send them, just because your grandfather did, and I appreciate that. I wanted to let you know that Nora and I will be there this year."

Susannah was clearly so astonished even her beautiful manners couldn't quite hide it. She managed a smile. "That's wonderful."

"Yeah, well… It just seemed…" The older man appeared to be looking for the right word. "It seemed like it was time."

Susannah nodded slowly. "I'm glad," she said. "I'll look forward to seeing you."

"Okay, then." Harrison gave a nod to Trent, then turned, steering his son toward the street, where his large black SUV gleamed in the sunlight, still sparkling from a fresh wash.

Trent watched them until their car disappeared at the end of Main Street. And then, to his surprise, he saw a Honda that looked a lot like Peggy Archer's pull out of a space down near the pet store and drive off in the same direction.

A small noise escaped Susannah's lips. "Was that Mrs. Archer?"

"I thought it might be. But maybe it's only because we just saw Harrison. Hondas are pretty common." He looked at her strained face. "Why?"

Susannah continued to gaze at the now-empty street, a small furrow between her eyebrows. "I don't know. I guess I was just surprised because I know she rarely comes back to Eastcreek."

It surprised Trent, too. He was well aware that Peggy had cut almost all ties with her hometown, except for the occasional visit to Paul's grave. She wouldn't even let Dr. Marchant treat her anymore, after a lifetime of his care.

He didn't mention any of that, of course. Instead, he tried to think how he could gracefully change the subject. He didn't intend to let the Archers destroy the fragile détente he'd achieved.

He was still sorting through the conversational universe, searching for a safe topic, when his cell phone rang. He had told everyone at the Double C to solve their own problems today, but the new hand had turned out to be a worrywart who always thought the world was ending when one of the horses sneezed or refused to eat.

It wasn't the Double C. It was, mystifyingly, Blanche Scovel, who lived next door to his father's cottage, where Trent had laid his head for the past five years. A retired librarian, Blanche was the perfect neighbor, a smart woman who minded her own business.

When he'd moved out to begin his year at Everly, he'd

given Blanche his cell number, confident she wouldn't dream of bothering him unless it was fairly important.

He considered holding out the phone so Sue could see the caller ID, too, but he knew she'd assume he was being sarcastic. So he simply answered it.

"Hi, Blanche. Everything okay?"

Susannah watched him carefully, her face impassive. He wondered whether she thought him capable of talking to Missy Snowdon in code names.

I don't lie anymore, Sue, he wanted to say. *It is possible for people to change.*

But what was the point?

He quietly listened to Blanche's news, which she delivered in typical no-nonsense fashion. In less than a minute, he had it all. He flipped shut the phone and turned to Susannah.

"I'm sorry, but I've got to go. That was my neighbor. She says there have been vandals at the cottage. If you'll give me a ride as far as the Double C, you can take the car back to Everly, and I'll grab a truck from the ranch."

"No." She frowned. "I'll go with you."

"You don't have time—"

"Trent." She put her hand on his arm. It lay there for maybe one second before she thought better of it and pulled it away. "Thanks to you, I do have time. I want to come."

He didn't argue. He didn't want to take the time.

Blanche hadn't provided many details, and as Trent drove he couldn't help imagining what form the vandalism might have taken. He hoped it wasn't major damage. Insurance would cover it, but he didn't have a spare second these days to oversee repairs.

It took only about seven minutes to get there. As they turned onto his street, Trent wondered if Susannah even remembered which house was his.

The Fugitive Four hadn't spent much time here. It wasn't snobbery that kept them away. It was just that a tiny house on a quarter-acre plot didn't offer enough places to hide from the watchful eyes of Trent's dad. Twenty thousand acres, on the other hand, gave hormone-driven teens all the privacy they craved.

Trent had bought the house from his dad a few years ago, when his dad made it clear he was eager to retire. It turned out great for both of them. Trent's dad got to take off and see the world, and Trent's investment paid off big-time. In the past few years, waterfront property had shot up, even when your water was just a creek so narrow you could spit across it, if you got some help from a decent wind.

From the street, everything looked okay—no visible damage. As he parked, he noticed Blanche standing on her porch. She was painting her shutters, covering the original dull green with a bright lavender.

Pretty soon, Trent's cottage would be the only one not updated with Easter egg pastels, which apparently were all the rage right now. His place was still an old-fashioned white with black shutters, just the way it had been when his dad lived here. His father was a compulsive gardener, so his color had come from the flowers, trees and vegetables that filled every square inch of the yard.

That was all gone, now. Trent was too busy to keep up with it all. And he didn't care much. His house was just a place to sleep.

Susannah paused after she shut the door, looking at the plain rectangles of grass that surrounded the house. She made a low, disappointed sound. "What happened to the roses?"

"I don't have time," Trent said. "The neighbors took some of them. The rest just died of neglect after Dad moved away, I'm afraid."

"What a shame," she said softly.

When Blanche saw them, she came to the railing, holding her paintbrush vertically so that she wouldn't drip blue on the yellow porch.

"The—well, the problem is in the back," she said. "It wasn't there yesterday, I'm sure. It must have happened last night, or while I was at the hardware store this morning."

"Thanks for the heads-up," Trent said. "We'll go take a look."

"I couldn't believe…" Blanche looked awkwardly from Susannah to Trent, hesitating.

Trent's antennae prickled. Uncertainty was rare for this sensible woman, whose thoughts always seemed to be as neatly organized as the rest of her life. "Well," she said finally. "I just wish I'd caught them, that's all."

Trent thanked her again, and he and Susannah walked around to the back, where the creek sparkled under the bright sunlight. He wasn't eager to take her into the house—not because he had so many sentimental leftovers from the past hanging around, but because he had so few.

With his dad's collections of dried plants, books and family albums all gone, the place looked more like a hotel room than a home. Neat, but sterile. Efficient, but oddly hollow.

It looked like the house of a man who was waiting to discover where he *really* belonged.

He didn't necessarily care to put that emptiness on display.

The mood was brighter out here, where a few hardy perennials had survived his neglect. Plumbago never died, and its blue flowers could handle summer heat. The watermelon-colored crape myrtle was just starting to bloom, and the waterside bank of lantana gold had spread another two feet since he'd been gone.

"Oh, this is beautiful," Susannah said happily. She ran her hand along the soft, white-flowered mounds of Indian hawthorne as they turned the corner. "Do you still have the firecracker plant? Were you able to keep the angelwing?"

Straightening, she shaded her eyes with her hand and scanned the backyard. Trent did, too, but for a different reason. He was looking for the vandalism, wondering what could have so upset his unflappable neighbor.

They both saw it at the same moment. Trent managed to react only with a tightening of his jaw, but Susannah gasped.

"Oh, Trent." She put her hand to her mouth. "Oh, no."

The clean white back of the house had been mutilated with blood-red spray paint. It looked as if it had been attacked by a slasher. And recently. The paint still glinted angrily in the sun.

BASTARD, the vandal had written in block letters to the left of the glossy black door.

And on the right he'd made his letters even larger, as if to emphasize his message.

MURDERER.

CHAPTER TEN

WHEN EVERLY LOOKED like this, with glass gleaming, silver sparkling and wood glowing with the contentment of a hundred years of care, Susannah remembered why she would do anything on earth to preserve the grand old dame.

The peach party was in full swing, and it was clear they had a success on their hands. The surly blond bombshell Trent had hired had turned out to be a hell of a housekeeper. When Trent and Susannah had got home that evening, after reporting the vandalism at the cottage to the sheriff, Everly had been spotless.

This morning, Imogene, Chase's housekeeper at the Double C, who was a genius with fresh flowers, had delivered a dozen huge arrangements of roses and daisies, and all the best blooms a Texas summer had to offer.

And, of course, all that cooking had paid off. An hour into the party, at least a hundred guests were milling around, inside the house as well as out back in the white tents overlooking the orchards.

Their plates were heaped with peach desserts, and it was funny to watch them trying to simultaneously chew and gush about how delicious everything was.

The favorite this year seemed to be the peach custard streusel pie, which was so fantastic it could make even Susannah's mouth water, though she had eaten enough peaches lately to last a lifetime.

"Great party," Richard Doyle said, strolling up with a champagne flute in each hand. "And you look magnificent. How about a birthday toast?"

She accepted the drink and the compliment—which couldn't possibly be true, given how tired she was—with a smile.

"Thanks. I'm sorry I haven't had any time to chat, but…" She sighed. She was mighty glad she'd decided to splurge on several waiters and a bartender. Otherwise she might have lost her mind.

"Even when you think you're prepared, there's so much to do." She scanned the living room, seeing several new arrivals who must have shown up while she was in the kitchen. "So many guests to talk to. I haven't seen some of these people since last year."

"It's a flattering turnout," Richard agreed, sipping his champagne, letting his gaze sweep over the crowd, too, though he couldn't have known many of the guests. "Your grandfather would be proud."

She watched him over the rim of her crystal flute. He was so good-looking…or, at least, he should have been. He had crisp leading man features, hair like spun gold, and an air of elegance you didn't often see in cowboy country.

She knew he had been interested in her ever since they met at the reading of her grandfather's will. She'd even wondered once, as they discussed details a few months later, whether he might be hinting that he'd like to serve as the husband she needed.

But that had felt oddly unethical—would he really suggest he help break a will he himself had written? And of course she could never marry a man she hardly knew. The risks were too great. Even the most ironclad prenup, as everyone knew, was just the starting point for divorce negotiations.

Most importantly, though, was that somehow she couldn't work up even the tiniest *poof* of chemistry when she was around him. He might as well have been a cardboard cutout of a movie star, for all the effect he had on her pulse.

"Oh, I'm sorry," she said, spying Harrison and Nora Archer entering the front hall. The pair looked awkward, as if they might back out again. "I see someone else I need to talk to. Please, help yourself to the streusel. It's fabulous."

She didn't look back to see whether he was annoyed. She set her flute on the nearest table and made a beeline for the door.

"Mr. Archer," she said. "I'm so glad you really could make it."

She smiled at Nora, a woman much closer to Susannah's age than to Harrison's. Tonight, the age difference between husband and wife was even more pronounced. Next to Nora's peaches-and-cream skin and bouncing red curls, Harrison looked gray, sour and just plain old.

Once again, Susannah was struck by how much Nora resembled a younger Peggy. It was almost obscene, and she frequently wondered how Nora could stand knowing she would always be the copy, never the original.

"Hi, Susannah." Though Nora was smiling politely, neither she nor her husband had moved a muscle, as if they'd just entered the lion's den. She glanced nervously up at Harrison, asking in spouse-code whether he intended to stay.

Hoping to prevent their departure, Susannah took Nora's arm and nudged her away from the door. "Won't you come in and taste some of the recipes? They're particularly good this year. And I see Fred Bollinger over there. I know he'd love to see you."

That was a bit of luck. Harrison and Fred were friends from way back, when they'd both made a killing on some land just south of town. Susannah finally saw the stiffness fall from Harrison's face as he spotted, then moved in to greet, his buddy.

"Thank you," Nora whispered, her eyes carefully watching her husband as he moved into the room. "I wasn't sure he'd actually be able to come. This is a hurdle he needed to jump, you know? He has to move past this…this baggage."

Susannah didn't respond. That was what people on the outside always said, that you were hanging on to old baggage, that you needed to get over it, forgive and forget, move on. They had no idea how pain and guilt and anger could live inside you, their throb becoming like a second heartbeat. You could go days without consciously thinking of them, but they were always there, and eventually you couldn't imagine life without them.

"He's a good man," Nora went on, her voice soft. "He deserves to be happy."

Susannah didn't know Nora well, but she'd often questioned whether the marriage could really be based on love. Harrison was such a stereotypical good-old-boy, with his bandy legs, puffed-out chest and avaricious eyes. As a child, she'd been a regular in his household, and she knew that he was chauvinistic, dictatorial and hard to please.

But the worried tenderness on Nora Archer's face certainly looked like love.

"Can I get you some champagne?" Susannah glanced around for a waiter with a tray of fresh flutes. "I'd be happy to—"

The front door opened again. Instinctively, Susannah turned, a welcoming smile on her face. Which of her guests wasn't here yet? She still hadn't heard from Jim Stilling, who was out of town on a case.

Maybe Dave Stanley and his daughter had decided to come after all?

But the person who walked through the door was one who absolutely had *not* been invited. It was someone who should have been miles and miles away.

"Nikki?"

Susannah's voice couldn't possibly have traveled all the way to Nikki's ears, but the younger girl glanced over, just as if she'd heard. She met her big sister's horrified gaze stubbornly, her eyebrows raised in an expression of insolent defiance she must have practiced ahead of time.

Oh, Lord. Susannah's chest tightened. The school was fifty miles away. How had Nikki managed to get here? Had she hitchhiked? Had she taken a bus? Could she possibly have saved enough money for a cab?

She was wearing too much makeup, naturally. She had cut her hair, and wore it spiked out. Her plaid skirt deliberately waged a war of aesthetics with her striped and wrinkled boy's shirt. She would have looked terrible even if she'd been going to a street fight. At a formal party, she looked...bizarre.

Susannah hurried over, her anger building. "What are you doing here? How did you get here?" She took Nikki's arm and pulled her into the shadowy alcove formed by the curve in the staircase. She tried to keep her voice low. "*Tell* me you didn't hitchhike."

Nikki shrugged. "Okay," she said, smiling with one side of her mouth. "I didn't hitchhike."

One, two, three... Susannah took a deep breath, hoping sanity would prevail.

"What are you doing here? Art school is not over for another month. I expressly told you that—"

"That what? That I wasn't welcome in my own home? That I couldn't be here for my own sister's birthday?" For the first time, Nikki's face looked her real age, a very mixed-up sixteen. Susannah remembered being that age, trying to face down her grandfather.

Her heart melted a little.

And of course Nikki caught the scent of vulnerability. She put on her best wheedling expression. "I haven't ever missed a peach party in my life, Susannah. Or your birthday. I couldn't miss this one. I just couldn't." She let her eyes get misty. "What are you going to do, throw me out?"

Susannah knew checkmate when she saw it. She glanced over her shoulder toward the guests, who hadn't seemed to notice Nikki's arrival. She made a quick decision.

"Okay, look. I'll make you a deal. If you want to be at this party so badly, go upstairs and make yourself look like a person who would have been invited. If you behave yourself, you can stay. I won't say another word tonight, and we can talk about…all this…in the morning."

Nikki grinned, leaned in and kissed Susannah on the cheek.

"Okay." She started to skip toward the stairs, turning at the last minute. "Oh, and there's a guy outside who needs a hundred-fifty dollars, okay? You'll recognize him. He's the one in the bright yellow car."

Susannah's eyes widened, and for a minute she thought she might run after her spoiled sister, drag her back out to the cab and give the driver a million bucks to dump her off the edge of the earth.

A hundred and fifty dollars? Didn't Nikki have a clue how many peaches you had to pick, with aching arms and stiff, stinging fingers, to net that much profit?

"I've got some cash on me," Trent said, suddenly appearing at her elbow. "I knew we might have to hire some cabs after all the champagne tonight, anyhow. Might as well start with this one."

Susannah turned to him and tried to smile. "Thank goodness you planned ahead." She pressed her fingers between her eyes. "Do you have any idea how many times in the past two days you've rescued me?"

"I guess I forgot to keep count." With a wink, he

reached into the pocket of his tuxedo, which, she noticed, looked absolutely fantastic, and pulled out some folded money. "Should we see if we can lower the price by throwing in a piece of the custard streusel?"

She wouldn't have thought she could laugh, this soon after the shock of seeing Nikki, but she did. She followed Trent out to the front, where a bored driver sat behind the wheel of his dusty cab in the oyster shell driveway.

Susannah knew she should stay inside and tend to her guests, but she needed a minute of privacy. Everyone else was either in the house or out back in the tents, admiring the view. She'd strung paper lanterns in the nearest rows of peach trees, and they looked like a fairy-tale land glimmering in the distance.

Out here, though the view was more prosaic, the air was cool, the moon was full, and the smell of the peaches wafted toward them, hanging in the air like unheard music. Surely it wouldn't be a social fatality to steal a minute or two.

She hung in the background, leaning against one of the porch's newel posts, until the cabbie peeled off, clearly annoyed at having been kept waiting. Trent made sure the man exited the property, then joined Susannah at the foot of the steps.

"That girl is a hard one to tame, isn't she?"

She sank onto the second step and sighed. "I'm starting to think it's impossible. She doesn't care about danger. She'll take any risk. When she wants something bad enough, she doesn't think twice. She just goes out and gets it, and damn the cost."

He smiled. "Sometimes that's called courage."

"Maybe. But it's never called wisdom. And it takes wisdom to stay safe."

He rested his arm on the post, his long-fingered hand dangling not far from her cheek. "You don't think safety might be just a little bit overrated?"

"Not for Nikki." She glanced up at the window to her little sister's room, where a light blazed for the first time in six weeks. "Not for anyone, really."

He knew what she was talking about, of course. He'd been there all those years ago when news came of her parents' car crash, and he'd been there throughout the next few difficult years while she tried to take on the role of Nikki's mother. He had watched her develop the protective anxiety that goes along with the job.

But he also knew that she bitterly regretted the one time in her own life when she'd acted on impulse, and the foolish mistake that had caused her world to explode around her.

They fell into an edgy silence. He had no intention of talking about any of that openly. Neither of them wanted to dredge up the whole business with Paul tonight, right in the middle of their truce. They'd even managed not to discuss the subject yesterday at his cottage, though the words scrawled on his walls were like a neon sign, pointing to Paul.

Who had written them, she wondered? The story was old but not forgotten in Eastcreek, so theoretically it could have been anyone. But she couldn't put that disturbing image of Peggy out of her mind. Peggy's unfocused eyes, her slurred voice saying, "I was watching you."

On the other hand, Trent hadn't seemed too worried. He'd simply observed that it wasn't surprising that their marriage had stirred up emotions. He'd calmly phoned the sheriff, and then he'd called someone from the Double C to paint over it.

Typical Trent. No muss, no fuss, always in control.

He sat down beside her on the steps. She didn't shift away, even when he brushed a small white jasmine bloom from her hair. But she did sigh, releasing some of the weariness of the past few weeks.

He reached out, took her face in his hand and lifted it to catch the porch light.

"You look like hell," he said.

She laughed. "Oh, really? I'll have you know this is my best dress." She lifted a flounce of the silky fabric, letting the gold threads wink in the moonlight. This had been her "best" dress for the past seven years, but it fit well enough that most men didn't care that it was slightly out-of-date.

Most men didn't even look above her neck.

She let the skirt fall, arranging it around her with a mock hauteur. "And Richard Doyle said I looked… I think the word he chose was *magnificent*."

Trent made a sound. "Richard Doyle is as slick as an oil spill. The dress is killer, and you know it. But your eyes look tired, Sue. I'll be glad when the party's over, and you can get some rest."

"Three days," she said, sighing just to think of it. "Three days off, and then the Redglobes need to be picked. And from there it's *goodbye sleep* until August."

"Damn it." He took her bare shoulders in his hands.

"Let me hire someone to take your place. Get out of the orchard and get some rest."

She shook her head. "I know you mean well, but it won't work like that. I need to be out there. I can keep people motivated, and I can spot problems better than anyone, even Zander. I know what needs to be done."

"Sue—"

She put her hand up and let it rest on his. "I'll be fine. I do this every year. It's crazy while it lasts, but it's my life. I love the orchard. I'm not afraid of hard work."

"But I want…"

He didn't finish the sentence. His gaze had dropped to her mouth, and she felt his fingers tighten on her shoulders.

Instantly, her blood began to sizzle. It was crazy, with a hundred people inside, with Nikki upstairs, with her hostess duties going untended, but she knew what he wanted, and she wanted it, too.

He leaned his head closer, his gaze still on her lips. She wasn't sure she could breathe. Strobelike images from the wine cellar, and from the shower, flashed through her mind. She suddenly felt like a powder keg, sitting too close to a flame.

"I want you, Susannah," he said, and he was so close his warm breath fanned her skin. She tilted her head, trying to make it easy for him, trying to make it happen.

But, as if the fates intervened to save her from herself, she heard Chase's truck pull up in the drive. He must have seen the two of them sitting there, because he rolled down his window and called out a cheery hello before he even killed the engine.

"Sorry we're so late, but Josie had to have her dress let out, and the damn seamstress didn't get done with it until—"

They heard a small scuffle and a muffled cry. "Hey, that hurt! Why shouldn't I tell them?" Chase smiled over at them again. "Sorry, Josie thinks she looks fat, which is ridiculous because—"

Susannah had jerked to her feet, as shocked and awkward as if she'd been caught murdering someone, instead of just preparing to kiss her husband. She felt exposed and embarrassed, though she wasn't sure why.

Trent, on the other hand, still sat on the step, looking ridiculously sexy but completely at ease.

Chase dropped his jaw. "Hey, wait a minute. Were you guys actually…?" He grinned. "You *were*."

He laughed, then turned to his wife. "They *were*."

"Chase," Josie said, though she was smiling herself. "Shut up."

"Yeah, Chase," Trent agreed smoothly as he finally got to his feet. He reached out to open the truck door, as if they'd been out here solely to play valet for the newlyweds. "Do us all a favor and *shut up*."

THE LAST GUEST didn't leave until one in the morning, when Trent called a cab and pretty much stuffed the drunken fool into it.

Chase and Josie didn't count as guests, of course. They stayed another hour, helping with cleanup, until Chase noticed the circles under Josie's eyes and went into expectant father panic, insisting on taking her home.

At two-thirty, Trent decided to patrol the grounds one

last time, just to be sure they hadn't overlooked anyone who might have passed out on the grass from a surfeit of great food and free champagne.

In Zander's office, where all the outdoor breakers were located, he flicked off the power to the paper lanterns, watching through the window as the rows of peach trees blinked out and disappeared, like the finale of a magician's act.

He heard crickets in the silence, and the irritable hoot of an owl, but nothing out of place. Everything felt right, and he decided to head back to the house.

But as he passed the barn, something nebulous tweaked at his senses. It was dark, as it should be, and it was completely quiet. So what was it? He stood, his hands in his pockets, and tried to figure it out.

Smoke. That was it. He smelled smoke. It was a dreaded scent on any working land, and though this was too faint to be an actual fire, an overlooked cigarette from a tipsy guest could smolder for hours before finally flashing into flame.

Besides, this didn't smell old. It smelled fresh. And there hadn't been any guests out here since midnight, over two hours ago. He stood completely still and stared at the barn. Sure enough, in a couple of minutes he heard the sound of muffled laughter, followed by the scratch and flare of a match.

He moved quickly, opening the door before the people inside had a chance to dart for cover. Moonlight knifed through the open door, its full glow bright enough to show him the whites of the girl's eyes and the burning red tip of the boy's cigarette.

Damn it all. It was Nikki and Eli Breslin. The little bastard had the cigarette in one hand, and Nikki Everly's breast in the other.

"Well," Trent said coldly. "What a surprise."

Nikki leaped back. The boy stared right at him, unfazed, and actually had the nerve to grin and take a long drag on his cigarette.

Nikki, on the other hand, wasn't looking at anyone. She was too busy trying to retie the bows that held up her evening gown.

Trent wondered how far this would have gone, if he hadn't caught them in time.

Susannah had been so pleased when Nikki meekly returned downstairs tonight, bathed and combed, her face washed and repainted with only some ladylike lip gloss. She had even chosen a sleeveless yellow dress that modestly reached her knees.

Susannah had clearly been proud of her dignified little sister, introducing her to everyone. But Trent, as a male, recognized the danger, and he hoped that Eli Breslin didn't somehow catch a glimpse of her.

This cool, perfumed young beauty would be far more tempting to men than the scruffy guttersnipe Nikki ordinarily appeared to be.

Now, with slivers of hay in her mussed hair, her dress askew, and the lip gloss smeared and kissed off, she looked exactly like what she was: jailbait.

Eli flicked the ashes from the end of his cigarette. He raised his eyebrows. "What can we do for you, Mr. Maxwell?"

"You can go home," Trent responded pleasantly. "I'm afraid the party's over."

Eli grinned. "Yours may be," he said. "I wouldn't know. I wasn't invited to that one. But I'm pretty sure *ours* is just beginning."

Eli lifted a bottle of beer from his side and knocked back a long swig. Trent hadn't seen the liquor, but it explained a lot. Eli was insulted to be left off the guest list, but he probably would have swallowed it except that the beer had lulled his self-preservation instincts to sleep.

Without the engaging, ass-kissing facade in place, the real Eli Breslin emerged. Arrogant and spiteful and amoral as hell.

Even Nikki looked uncomfortable at his naked disrespect. She risked a look at Trent from under her eyebrows, then turned to Eli.

"Maybe I should go," she mumbled, toeing the hay.

"Suit yourself." The boy wiped his mouth with the back of his hand. "But he's not your dad, is he? What can he do?"

"He can tell my sister."

"Ooooh." Eli drew the sound out rudely. "Tell your *sister?* You really are a baby, aren't you? Too bad they let you grow boobs before you grow a spine."

Trent felt his heart beating up around his ears, and red sparks flashed at the edges of his vision. His right hand curled into a fist, but somehow he kept it at his side.

Oh, yeah, this kid was asking for it.

In the old days, Trent would simply have punched the little bastard. But he'd learned eleven years ago that the smallest act of violence, even one that felt completely justified at the time, could take on a life of its own. And you could end up losing a lot more than your temper.

He had sworn he'd never make that mistake again.

Somehow he kept his voice even. "Susannah is in the kitchen, Nikki. If you slip in the front door right now, she won't see you."

The girl hesitated. God, hormones were powerful, weren't they? Even after Eli's last comment, she didn't want to lose face in front of him. She didn't want to prove herself a child by letting Trent boss her around.

He let it go, aware that further pushing would only make things worse. The problem wasn't really Nikki, anyhow.

"Here's the deal, Breslin." He took out his cell phone. "I'm going to give you thirty seconds to take that booze, that cigarette, and your filthy ass out of this barn. Then I'll give you another thirty seconds to get off this property. Maybe two hours to get out of Eastcreek altogether."

Eli spit on his fingers, then snuffed out his cigarette between his thumb and forefinger, a trick he'd probably spent months perfecting. "And if I don't?"

Trent flipped open the phone. "If you don't, you're going to find out what happens to men over eighteen who put their dirty hands on underage girls."

"Oh, yeah? Like she didn't *want* me to."

Trent smiled. "Like that matters."

Eli stared at him, clearly trying to cut through the brain fog and figure out what to do.

"Oh, sorry," Trent said, starting to press the numbers of Zander's private line. "I forgot. Your brain obviously isn't working very well tonight."

The phone began to ring. Zander answered quickly, as a good foreman always did.

"Hey," Trent said. "Can you come out to the barn for a minute? Eli Breslin just quit, and he needs someone to help him find his way to the bus station. He's been drinking, and, as you know, he's pretty stupid even when he's sober."

That was all the humiliation the kid could take. Without so much as a goodbye glance at Nikki, he charged through the barn door, shouldering Trent aggressively as he passed.

Then he disappeared into the night.

Trent didn't bother to try to stop him. Zander would catch him as he gathered his things. The old foreman was a savvy man. Trent had complete faith that the boy would be on a bus by dawn.

He turned to Nikki.

"Look," he said, "I know we haven't seen much of each other in a long time, and you've probably heard a lot of bad things about me. But you're just going to have to take my word for this. Your sister is dog tired, and she doesn't need this kind of crap. Not ever. But definitely not tonight."

He'd half expected a sullen comeback, but Nikki just stared at the ground.

"Do you get what I'm saying?"

She didn't look up. "You're saying you're not going to tell her."

Well, that certainly cut to the chase. She apparently wasn't as dumb as she looked.

"That's right. I'm not going to tell her, not because I don't think you need a good thrashing, but because she's too tired to give it to you."

She shifted her shoulders. "She's *always* too tired. To tired to pay any attention to me, anyhow. That's why she sent me off to school, you know."

He shook his head, irritated. "*Spare me.* You want her attention, be where she is. Do what she does. Climb up on a ladder with her and pick some peaches. Get out a calculator and help her balance the books. Better yet, go get a towel right now and help her dry some of those dishes."

Nikki finally looked at him. Her pout had disappeared. "It's almost three. She's still cleaning up?"

"That's right. I don't know how she's even standing, but she's still cleaning up."

Nikki hesitated one more minute, fiddling with her spaghetti straps. Then she nodded slowly.

"Okay," she said. "I guess I can help."

He watched her all the way to the kitchen door. And, though he had planned to go in there himself, sweep Susannah off her tired feet and carry her up to bed, he let Nikki take his place.

Susannah had been happy tonight. And he'd give up anything to make sure she stayed that way.

CHAPTER ELEVEN

TRENT BUNKED on Susannah's sofa that night and didn't sleep much, even though Zander sent a text around five to say that he'd personally driven Eli into Austin and bundled him onto a Greyhound back home to the Panhandle.

Good riddance.

Still, Trent felt edgy, plagued by a vague sense that being unconscious might be a mistake. He lay there, trying to figure out what had him so restless, but nothing made much sense. Lots of little glitches had come along, from the vandalism at the cottage to the mess with Nikki and Eli. But nothing that warranted a twenty-four-hour vigil over Everly.

When the sun finally struggled up over the horizon, revealing the beginnings of another beautiful day, he accepted that he was single-handedly turning innocent molehills into mountains. He had work waiting at the Double C, and he might as well get to it.

On the way off the property, he stopped by Zander's office and asked him to keep an eye on things. Thankfully, the older man didn't ask why, since Trent didn't really have a good answer. It just made him feel better, that was all.

When he reached his own office at about seven, he instinctively breathed a metaphorical sigh of relief. The ranch manager's building, an attractive brick structure shaded by the orange-yellow flowers of a cassia tree, looked like an oasis.

It would be nice for a change to work with the best tools, equipment and men. The Double C was the best-run ranch in central Texas, not because Trent was such a brilliant manager, but because the Claytons had a zillion dollars and no passions to blow it on except their land and their horses.

As he got out of the Mercedes and fingered the key ring to lift free the one that opened the office door, he heard another car pull up behind him.

He turned, hoping it was Chase, because he was the only person who wouldn't take offense if Trent ordered him to get lost.

Was it too much to ask for a few minutes of privacy? He didn't want to socialize with the vet, he didn't want to mediate a dispute between ranch hands, and he damn sure didn't want to buy a new copy machine from some eager beaver door-to-door type.

Just let it be Chase.

Of course, that would have been too easy. It wasn't Chase. Instead, it was Trouble. Capital *T.*

It was Missy Snowdon.

From the forgiving distance of a few yards, she looked damn good. She still had that amazing body and crazy blond hair that looked pretumbled, as if she'd just climbed out of bed and couldn't wait to get back in it. With you.

But as she came closer, with that undulating walk he

remembered so well, he saw that the years had strangely altered her angel face.

A whole decade had passed, of course, since they'd met face-to-face. People aged. None of them, not even Susannah, had been floating untouched in fairyland.

But this was different.

Missy's skin was taut and shiny, as if she had scrubbed and peeled and frozen it in place so often it was more like plastic than human flesh. Her sensual lips were almost comically swollen now, like the mouth on a cartoon vixen.

The effect wasn't ugly, but it was too artificial to be even remotely sexy. It was almost as if her face had been taken apart and then put back together just a hair wrong. He wondered for a moment whether she might have been in some kind of accident, but then he realized what had really happened.

She'd begun to wage the war on aging so early and so compulsively that she'd lost sight of the natural beauty she'd been blessed with. At only thirty. *Good God.*

"Well, hello, stranger." She hitched her slouchy purse over her bare, bony shoulder. She wore what looked like riding jodhpurs and a white shirt tied off at the midriff, exposing a hollow stomach and ribs he could count.

She'd lost a hell of a lot of weight. She'd always been trim, but now everything on her was angular, except for the helium-balloon breasts and the blowfish lips.

Poor kid. She'd always had self-esteem issues, hadn't she? Probably that was why she had enjoyed stealing boyfriends—it made her feel powerful. He'd been such a horny moron he had thought she actually had the hots for him, which had, pathetically, played right into his own self-esteem issues.

What a couple of desperate losers they had been, pretending to be so cool.

He fought the urge to look away. It wasn't her fault she reminded him of a Trent he was ashamed to have been.

"Hi, Missy," he said. "How are you? It's been a long time."

"Too long." She licked her lips. "But we can fix that."

"Missy—"

"What do you say we go for an early-morning ride? I know some quiet places along the creek. We could...get to know each other again."

He shook his head gently. "I'm married, remember? Any riding I do these days better be with my wife."

"With her? Or on her?" She smiled, catlike, blinking slowly. Her eyelids didn't quite move in sync. He belatedly registered that her perfume was mixed with another scent.

Only seven in the morning, and she was already drunk.

He tried to keep the disgust off his face, but he must not have been completely successful. She tossed her hair across one shoulder and chuckled. "Don't be such a bore, Trent. If that coldhearted nag is your only mount these days, you're missing all the fun."

The vulgarity didn't even make him mad. Ten years ago, he'd thought the bitchy put-downs that issued out of her rosebud mouth were perversely sexy. He—and all the other boys—had encouraged her, had made her believe that rich little beauty queens who acted like sluts were the ultimate turn-on.

"Missy, listen to me. I want to make this very plain. I'm not just playing hard-to-get here. I cheated on Susannah once, and made an unbelievable mess of things. I'm not going to do it again."

She narrowed her eyes and tilted her head. "Have you forgotten how good it was, Trent?"

"No, but—"

Suddenly, more like a monkey pouncing than anything else, she jerked forward, took his head between her hands, and pulled him down for a kiss.

If this was her idea of seduction, she'd completely lost her touch.

She ground against him for a few seconds, trying to get a response. She pushed her tongue into his mouth. He could taste the liquor as well as the mouthwash she'd used to try to hide it.

Gently, he eased her away. He didn't want to hurt her. It was clear she already was hurting about as much as anyone he'd ever known.

"Missy, come on. You don't really want to do this. You are so much better than this—"

She reached up and slapped him.

Man, she packed a punch. His cheek was going to sting for a while.

"How dare you?" she said. "How dare you give me that sanctimonious crap?"

She was breathing hard, and her eyes were lined red, though her facial muscles were so rigid from BOTOX or whatever that she wasn't able to crumble like a normal woman.

"Don't you *dare* tell me what I want. How can you

know anything about it? I do want this." She gulped for air. "I want *someone*. Everyone wants someone, Trent."

She began to cry. Heaven help him, this wasn't an act. There was no attempt to ration diamond tears daintily, to pluck any chivalric strings he might still possess.

It was bizarre, watching fat, painful streams fall when her brow remained unfurrowed. The tears ran down her shiny cheeks and pooled in the corners of her twisted mouth.

And *great*...now they had an audience, as the ranch came alive for the day. Cowboys and ranch hands strolled to and from the stables. Even that damn copier salesman Trent had predicted had arrived and was standing beside his open car door, looking uncertain.

Missy put her face in her hands, rested her head against his chest and continued to cry. Loudly.

Goddamn it.

He'd rather deal with a dozen Eli Breslins than one sloppy-drunk ex-lover.

Still, much as he might want to, Trent couldn't just pour her back into her car and hope the tears and the booze didn't send her careening into a tree—or worse, into some unsuspecting mom ferrying her kids to school.

Goddamn it.

What a day! He enjoyed a beer like any other red-blooded Texan, but if he ran into one more person all liquored up and out of control, he was going to join the Temperance League.

Waving the salesman away with one hand, he put his arm around Missy and led her toward his office.

As he reached the door, he saw Josie coming up the sidewalk, carrying a carafe of hot coffee and a bag of muffins. She must have seen his car. They often had breakfast together these days, so that Trent could teach her about her new husband's ranch.

About ten feet away, she hesitated. Her eyes widened as she looked at the sobbing female in Trent's arms. She started to rush forward, automatically assuming the woman must need help.

Trent shook his head emphatically. Missy had never liked other women, and she didn't look as if she'd embraced the Girl Power Sisterhood over the past few years. God only knew what kind of scene she would stage if Josie said something she considered patronizing.

Josie stopped again, frowning. She watched him, clearly waiting for a signal.

Thank God for smart women.

Call Chase, he mouthed over Missy's head.

And then, praying he wasn't making the second-biggest mistake of his life, he unlocked the door and ushered her in.

An hour later, when Chase put Missy in his truck, started the engine and eased off down the drive, Trent finally let go of the breath he didn't realize he'd been holding.

She was gone, and Chase had done such a good job of sweet-talking her that she probably wouldn't ever come back. Heck, Chase had been so charming that by the end Missy had been crying all over again, this time for Trent and his poor broken heart.

When she'd left, pumped full of black coffee and Chase's ego-soothing baloney, she'd even apologized for kissing him and wished him good luck with his marriage.

Trent opened the door to his inner office, glad that he wouldn't eternally have to carry the picture of Missy Snowdon sitting on the other side of his desk, weeping without moving a single facial muscle. Chase had worked his miracles in the anteroom, where Trent's secretary would have been sitting, if Josie hadn't phoned her and warned her to come in late.

Trent flicked on his computer and took a sip of leftover coffee while he waited for it to boot up. Too bad he didn't have Chase Clayton IV's magic touch with women. His problems with Susannah would have disappeared in a puff of happy-dust years ago.

But Trent was not Mr. Sunshine. And Susannah wasn't as simple, or as sad, as Missy Snowdon.

Besides, there was no telling what would happen once Missy was back at home and free from Chase's mind-altering bliss-vibes. She'd probably pick up another vodka tonic and drink herself back into the same mess by midnight.

Only maybe this time she'd start stalking Chase, instead. Trent smiled as he sat down at his desk. Now that would be funny.

He worked in idyllic silence awhile, letting the ranch business fill his mind with easy problems that had neat, predictable answers.

But after about ten minutes, he heard something odd.

He listened. And then, in the silence, he felt a subtle movement by his feet.

The hair on the back of his neck prickled.

Something was in the knee well of his desk.

Using an instinct developed from years of interacting with the land, he went completely still. So did the thing at his feet.

Barely turning his head, he surveyed the room, looking for a weapon. Something long…like a shovel. He wanted to be wrong, but the primitive part of his brain had already processed what the mysterious movement had to be.

The snake that lay coiled at his feet might be completely innocent, a black racer trying to escape the heat, or a harmless garter snake who had mistaken the darkness of the desk for a makeshift cave.

Or it could be a killer. A rattler or a copperhead, with fangs full of venom and an instinct to attack.

For another second, he continued to scan the room, hoping. But Trent's quarters weren't part of a barn office, like Zander's, and no heavy tools lay around, waiting for repairs. His was slick and civilized, and the closest thing to a weapon was a quartz paperweight his dad had given him when he'd come home from California.

No good. Useful for bashing in the head of a human intruder, maybe. But he'd never get the thing near a snake before its fangs were buried in his flesh.

He had only one choice, and it was a crummy one. But it got crummier with every second that passed, so he didn't wait.

He took a deep breath, and then he slid the chair back slowly, so slowly it hardly seemed to be moving.

Once again, he found himself holding his breath. But nothing flashed from the knee well. Nothing sank into his calf.

When he was completely free of the desk, he eased up from the chair and stepped back, making no noise, jostling no furniture, ruffling no papers, until he was at least ten feet from whatever lay beneath.

First he began to breathe again. Then he used his cell to make a call to the stables, and quietly told the answering ranch hand to send Boss Johnson over ASAP with a snake pole and a net.

Finally, he pulled out his pocket flashlight and aimed its beam into the shadows.

Cold fingers played up and down his spine.

The hourglass shape was unmistakable. Coiled in the corner of the knee well was a twenty-inch copperhead.

Its tail was vibrating, so it wasn't a happy fellow, but apparently Trent's caution had kept it from feeling molested enough to strike.

After a few seconds, the door opened, not loudly. Boss Johnson stuck in his head. "Where is it?"

"Under the desk."

"What is it?"

"Copperhead."

Boss Johnson came quietly around the desk. Trent moved his flashlight once again over the shadows.

The older man whistled. He looked at Trent, his eyes squinted into slits. "Did you sit at that desk?"

"Yes."

"How come you're still alive?"

"Dumb luck, I guess." Trent took the pole from the other man. They'd relocated a dozen snakes together since Trent had taken over as manager, and they made a pretty good team. "Ready?"

But the trainer's eyes were still narrowed. He scanned the room, much as Trent had done earlier, but they both knew he wasn't looking for a weapon. He was looking for an opening. A broken window, a compromised door. A cracked attic vent, a piece of rotting wood.

But nothing like that ever existed on the Double C.

"Damn it, Maxwell," the man said in a low, troubled voice. "We're asking the wrong questions."

"And the right one is?"

"How the hell did this guy get in here?"

SUSANNAH HAD TO EAT some serious crow to get the school director to let Nikki come back. But she'd succeeded. Now if she could only get Nikki to cooperate.

"It's just another month," she said as she slid into the driver's seat of her car and inserted the key into the ignition. She rolled down the window. "You'll be home by late July."

Nikki laid her hands on the window frame and tilted her head down to peer into the car. She scuffed the dirt with her shoe.

"A month," she said, "is a long time."

Frustrated, Susannah looked at her watch. She'd stayed several hours, touring the school and trying to make Nikki feel better about staying. She wasn't about to let all those tuition dollars go to waste, and she wasn't about to bring Nikki back to the sizzling cauldron of emotion that Everly had become since Trent moved in. So she'd met her sister's friends and spent at least an hour looking at her portfolio of watercolors, which were actually quite good.

Some of the paintings were of places on Everly property and sentimentally rendered. Susannah was amazed that Nikki loved anything about her home enough to recreate it from memory.

However, the shadows from the school's spreading oaks were long now, stretching across the pretty adobe mission buildings. If Susannah didn't leave in the next half hour, it would be dark when she got home, and she still had a hundred things to do.

She sighed and ran her hand through her hair. "A year ago you insisted you'd die if you didn't come to this school."

"And you said we couldn't afford it."

"We couldn't. But I found a way, because *you* said you couldn't bear to hang around for my *farce* of a wedding."

She was glad to see that Nikki had the grace to look embarrassed about that. It had definitely been one of her brattiest moments.

"The money's spent now, Nikki, and we can't get it back. So you might as well enjoy the school. See if you can learn something, so it's not a total waste."

The words weren't meant to be harsh, just realistic. But all of a sudden, in the sharpening light, Nikki's eyes looked oddly wet.

Damn it. Why, just when they seemed to be making a little progress toward being buddies, did Susannah always have to return to the role of The Enforcer? She was only fourteen years older than Nikki. She didn't have all the answers. God, her own life was an even bigger mess than Nikki's was.

Susannah forced herself to stay strong. She was the only parent figure Nikki had ever known, except for the cold, sternly distant presence of their grandfather. Susannah had clung to the job of mothering her little sister when it was easy, refusing to accept that Nikki could ever need anything more. If she gave up now, just because Nikki had hit the squalls of adolescence, then she really would have done her little sister a profound injustice.

Susannah's cell phone, which she'd dumped on the passenger seat, rang. She looked at the screen, hoping it would be an Austin area code. She had put a call in to the SuperPantry headquarters, checking to see if their East-creek locations could handle any more peaches this season.

She needed them to say yes. She was desperate for outlets.

It was the difference between salvation and wretched failure. *Please, let it be the store, and let them say yes....*

But it wasn't Austin. It wasn't the miracle she'd been praying for.

It was Nell Bollinger. Immediately, Susannah's conscience sent up a guilty signal. *Darn it.* She, Nell and Josie had been planning to assemble donation baskets of peaches for the local nursing homes and hospitals. It wouldn't put any money in the Everly coffers, but it would be a worthy cause.

And anything was better than letting the beautiful fruit rot.

Caught in the mess with Nikki, Susannah had forgotten entirely, hadn't even phoned to cancel. She groaned inwardly, but let the call go to voice mail. Nikki always complained that she couldn't have a five-minute conversation with Susannah without Everly orchard business interfering.

Susannah would focus on Nikki now. Then, as soon as she got on the road, she'd phone Nell and make her apologies.

"Nik, honey. I really do have to go."

Nikki nodded. "I know. It's just—" she squeezed the door frame so hard her knuckles paled "—I feel bad. Obviously you need all the help you can get. With the peaches, I mean."

Susannah let one corner of her mouth ride up. They both knew Nikki hated picking peaches and found imaginative ways to get out of it nine days out of ten.

"I know what you're thinking." The younger girl blushed, which surprised the heck out of Susannah. Nikki had probably been about five years old the last time Susannah had seen her show real shame about her behavior. "I'll do better this year, really. I promise."

Susannah put her hand over Nikki's. "I appreciate that, kiddo. But July and August are always hectic, and the Jersey Queens are going to go crazy this season. Believe me, there will be plenty to do when you get back."

Nikki nodded again, obviously recognizing that she had run out of ways to postpone the inevitable. She squared her shoulders, then leaned in through the window and kissed Susannah quickly on the cheek.

This time it was Susannah's eyes that grew moist.

She fiddled with the steering wheel, trying to swallow the lump in her throat. She couldn't remember the last time Nikki had kissed her.

They said goodbye. Susannah thought about telling Nikki she loved her, but decided not to push her luck. A blush, a kiss and an offer to pick the Dixielands... that was a lot for one day.

As she turned onto the highway, her heart felt lighter than it had in months.

Yes, there were a hundred things to do, a million bills to pay...but she'd get through. She always did.

The trees looked a little like Nikki's watercolors, blurring slightly as they streaked past, the golden sunset gilding the summer green. It was a gorgeous day, and maybe, before it was over, she'd get that yes from SuperPantry.

She glanced at the phone. *Oh, yeah.* It wasn't all bliss and optimism. She still needed to call Nell.

She decided to listen to the message first. It wouldn't hurt to know exactly how ticked her friend was. Nell did, after all, have the infamous Bollinger temper.

The woman's first words didn't sound furious, which was a good sign. Nell didn't mince words...or anything else. When she was mad, she knew how to light into you with a vocabulary that would make the toughest ranch hand cringe.

"Susannah, honey, this is Nell. I hope everything's okay. Josie and I were waiting for you for quite a while, and... Well, here's the thing. When I went to pick up Josie at the Double C, I..."

Several seconds of rustling noises filled the airwaves, and then came the sound of Nell clearing her throat.

"Well, damn it, I'm just going to say it. I saw Trent standing out there, in broad daylight, with Missy Snowdon, old Roger Snowdon's oldest, you know, the trashy one. And…I guess I thought you ought to know. He was kissing that girl like a pig eats an apple."

CHAPTER TWELVE

IT TOOK HER FOREVER to find him.

She checked the Double C first, but his car wasn't there, so she didn't even stop. The last thing she needed was to run into Chase. Loyal to a fault, he'd make up a hundred ridiculous rationalizations for anything his best friend might have done.

And Susannah was sick of excuses.

From there, she went by the Snowdon spread, though it dragged her another ten miles east, which was not smart. It was getting late. The night, like a cloudy bully, had already shoved the sunset down into one narrow stripe of the sky.

The Snowdon mansion dominated a small hill, from which velvet green paddocks spread out in all directions. The front driveway circled a gushing fountain, at which the Snowdons' luxury vehicles were parked, modern-day black stallions nosing up to the trough.

If Trent's Mercedes had been among them, Susannah would have seen it a quarter mile away. But it wasn't. And under her fury she could feel the tiny wash of relief, which only made her mad at herself, as well as at Trent.

Was she such a fool that even now she was hoping it wasn't true?

She turned for home, driving a little too fast, partly due to angry adrenaline, partly to a desire to beat the darkness and rain.

The minute she arrived, she saw his car. He'd come home, then. And why not? He had no idea his infidelity had been witnessed…or reported. He might even be hoping that, having played the knight in shining armor so well for the past few days, he could reap his reward tonight.

Well, he wasn't completely wrong. If she had anything to say about it, he was going to get *exactly* what he deserved.

Before she exited the truck, Zander loped up, dodging the first of the fat drops of rain.

"I was just heading home," he said. "We put a couple of extra guys on today and got most of the ripe fruit off the trees. Everything else is still pretty green. The rain may pass over, but even if it doesn't, I don't think it will hurt us much."

"Thanks," she said, though, for the first time in a long time, the future of the peaches was not her first priority. "Have you seen Trent?"

"Yeah." Zander wiped his face with his handkerchief. "He picked with us most of the afternoon. You think he'd be worn-out, but after that he went out on the western border."

That was not what she'd expected to hear. "Why?"

"Trim some trees, he said. I thought I'd heard wrong, but he took the key for the shed." He shook his head.

"He's still not back. Did you guys fight or something? He's been like a prickleburr all day. And asking every few minutes whether I'd heard from you."

"Thanks." The heavily treed western border, which used to be a windbreak back when those outermost acres were producing, was too far to walk. She turned over the ignition and pulled away, leaving Zander watching, obviously confused.

She was pretty confused, herself. Why on earth would Trent have decided to tackle such a tough job so late in the day? She knew that a lot of the old Ponderosa's loblollies, elms and oaks needed cleaning up, but Zander was right. No one in his right mind would start such a task after an afternoon picking peaches in the heat.

But maybe a man who wanted to be alone would.

Or maybe *alone* wasn't the right word.

Maybe *private* would be better.

She growled, ripping the truck over the unpaved shortcut, her teeth knocking together as the old shock absorbers tried to manage the bumps. If Trent Maxwell was using the woods on her western border to make wild outdoor love to that dirty Missy Snowdon, Susannah would...

Well, she didn't know what she'd do. But it wasn't going to be pretty.

She parked at the toolshed, a half-dilapidated structure where they kept some old equipment. The shed was unlocked, the door half-cocked.

When she looked inside, though, she saw nothing but an old mower, a tiller and a couple of bags of organic fertilizer that had begun to smell pretty rank.

She wrinkled her nose. Even Missy Snowdon would probably draw the line at making love here.

Susannah backed out, shut the door and walked toward the trees. As she did, she heard twigs cracking and leaves being brushed about. She hesitated briefly, wondering whether she might be about to confront a wild turkey, or a fox or a deer, instead of the more common pest—the cheating husband.

So what? She began moving again, following the noises, not caring what they turned out to be. In this mood, she could burst in on a grizzly bear, and the bear would be the one who ought to be afraid.

She almost missed him. He was working on a dead pine stump, about five yards off the path.

In there, the thick overhead canopy of branches almost completely shut out the blue-and-purple twilight. He had taken his shirt off, and the bronze gleam of his chest was the only part of him visible in the shadows.

The chain saw lay on the ground beside the stump. He was dragging a large loblolly branch toward a pile of broken twigs and needles, and he clearly hadn't heard her arrive.

Missy wasn't here. Once Susannah knew that, she didn't stop to think. She picked her way past the low-hanging branches and met him inside the wood.

When he saw someone coming, he looked up from his labors, his sweaty, bare shoulders tensing. But even when he recognized her, he didn't fully relax.

"What is it?" His voice sounded harsh. "Is something wrong?"

She folded her arms, grabbing her elbows. "Oh, yeah, I think you could say there's something wrong."

He dropped the heavy branch onto the pile. As it crashed into the others, it sent up a gust of pine-scented dust and mulch. He wiped his gloved hands on his jeans. "What is it? Are you okay?"

That was cute. Was she okay? No, she was far from okay. She hadn't been okay in eleven years, not since the first time he did this to her.

"I don't need to tell you what it is, do I? I think you know."

He looked at her hard for a moment, a deep furrow between his eyebrows. Then he wiped a trickle of sweat from his forehead, leaving behind a dirty smudge.

"Susannah, I cannot tell you what a crappy day I've had. I am not in the mood for mind games. If you've got something to say, say it."

"All right, I will."

She squared her shoulders. All the way out here, she'd been forbidding herself to cry. She wasn't a weeper. Now that she was actually in his presence, though, she didn't feel the least urge to shed tears. It would be far more satisfying to punch him in the nose.

"What's *wrong* is that you've started seeing Missy Snowdon again. What's wrong is that you're humiliating me in front of everyone I know. What's wrong, Trent, is that if you think I'm going to let you cheat on me again, after all these years, with the same boozy tramp, then you're as dumb as that loblolly stump."

He listened to the whole thing patiently, seemingly unfazed by her fury. When her tirade was over, he shook his head slowly. Then he took a moment to lazily arch his back, as if his muscles hurt.

When he straightened, he gave her a lopsided smile, nodding slightly.

"The grapevine has been busy, I see. I wonder which one of your friends it was." He extracted a pine needle that had found its way inside his glove. "Hey, you don't happen to know a copier salesman named Pete, do you?"

"What difference does it make who told me?" A momentary weakness pinched at the back of her eyes, making them threaten to water. "Obviously you're not denying it."

He shrugged. "What good would that do? Would you believe me?"

"Not for a second. Not for a millionth of a second. I didn't come out here to see if you'd deny it. I came out here to tell you it's going to have to stop."

"Oh, really?" He smiled again, but this time she sensed a tension beneath the carefully orchestrated posture of nonchalance. She sensed something slightly... dangerous.

"Really. I'm keeping my end of the bargain, and by God, you're going to have to keep yours. I'm giving you—"

She frowned, distracted by the way perspiration teased tiny glistening tracks through the wood chips and dirt on his chest. "I'm giving you—"

"What?" He rubbed a palm over his stomach, wiping the moisture away, apparently utterly unaware of how sexy the gesture looked. "What are you giving me?"

"I'm giving you everything you asked for. First in the cellar, and then, the other night, in the shower, I—" she tightened her arms across her chest "—I'm giving you everything you want."

"Everything I want?" He laughed, and the sound echoed in the dome of trees. "You can't possibly believe that, Susannah, so don't even say it. I told you. I'm not in the mood for more games."

"I'm giving you all I can." She heard a low ferocity thrumming in her voice. "How could I ever…completely…"

He waited, as still as one of the trees around him, for the rest of her sentence. She could barely make out his features now, as darkness claimed the wood.

"Why would I make any part of myself, body or heart or soul, vulnerable to a bastard like you?"

It was frightening, waiting for him to react. It was as if civilization was slipping away…not only his, but hers, too.

"Why?"

He cursed once, low, under his breath.

"I'll tell you why." Without warning, he reached out and grabbed her arm with his rough-gloved hand. He pulled her toward him, up against his bare chest. She was so close she felt wood chips scrape her skin.

Not knowing, or more likely not caring that he was transferring the earthy dirt from his body to hers, he bent his head and touched his lips to her throat. Her heart beat its wings and tried to fly away.

"You'll do it because, bastard or not, you want me."

She lifted her chin, searching for air, but all her lungs

could find was Trent, a sensual potpourri of sweat and dirt and danger.

"I don't. I don't want you."

"Maybe not," he growled. "But you *need* me."

He grabbed one edge of her blouse, a stretch-cotton fitted dress shirt that had looked so crisp and sensible at the school meeting this morning. With one deft twist of his wrist, he pulled free the long row of snaps.

Nothing tore, no fasteners clattered to the ground, but the act was a statement—a thrilling declaration of intent. And then, with those gloved hands that felt so strange, he reached inside her bra and found her aching breast.

"You need me as much as I need you," he said. "We're through keeping score and playing games. This isn't about Missy Snowdon, and it isn't about Paul. Tonight, it's about you and me. Tonight, it's about the truth."

She opened her mouth, but she never uttered a word. His mouth swooped down and closed over her lips, owning the very breath she exhaled.

This was more than a kiss. It was more passion, more unleashed need, than she'd ever known in her life. Her desire rose to meet his. His lips demanded, and her lips obeyed. His hands stroked, and her body wept with pleasure.

She didn't even try to stop it. It was like standing at the edge of a forest fire, too paralyzed, too hypnotized, to run.

The trees and the rain seemed to fold around them, locking them in a wet darkness that was both primitive and powerful. As if they were two savages who possessed no words, who required no explanations, he pulled her to a clear space, where the ground was crudely carpeted with green and brown needles.

She lay down, hot and hungry and oddly unashamed.

He pulled off his gloves, and as he undressed her, she tore at his jeans, desperate to feel the heat and the power her body remembered so well.

Finally, she was naked, and he was naked, and his hands were everywhere. She began to shiver, and he lowered himself over her, stopping just inches from her skin. His wet hair fell in her face as he kissed her breasts, and she clutched his arms, her fingernails digging into his skin.

He pressed himself against her, pushing once, then twice, teasing the secret part of her that melted and begged to be breached.

"Yes?" His eyes gleamed in the darkness.

"Yes," she answered. "Yes."

He lifted her hips, completing the puzzle with a slow, deliberate thrust. She cried out in the voice of the trees. Night birds lifted to the sky, startled.

He waited, giving her time to accept him. But soon she shifted her body, seeking more. And then finally, he was moving inside her, filling that fiery, aching emptiness that she had endured for so many years. She couldn't get enough. She held on to his hips, trying to take him deeper, trying to erase the line between her flesh and his.

He belonged inside her, rigid and full against her pulsing warmth. With him there, all the things she thought she had lost returned to her.

Suddenly she was whole again, a woman on the edge of a miracle.

"Help me, Trent," she said, and his body answered. His rhythm was masterful, slowly building. She began to pant as something coiled inside her.

"Yes," she whispered, as he pulled her breast into his hot mouth. His hips moved faster, then faster still, plunging the light and the fire into the deepest, most secret places she possessed.

This was the truth he had been talking about. The truth about her own body, her own soul. He had come through the darkness, and he had found her. She was a cave of melting diamonds. She was a million sparks, helplessly flashing and glittering, held together only by his hands.

He lifted her legs again, higher, braiding them around his neck, and it was almost too much. She heard herself whimpering, felt herself pulsing and pushing and arcing.

And finally, oh, yes…going up in beautiful flames.

When it was over, her mind cleared slowly. The starlight in her body dimmed, eclipsed and finally grew cold.

He lay on his back beside her, his breath still heavy and loud in the silence. She stared up into the pines and found a single faraway star between the clouds, and waited for him to speak.

But he didn't, though she waited until long after his breath began to ease. She waited until a cloud smothered the star. Until the damp earth against her back sent a shiver into her soul.

Of course, her aching heart told her. Of course he didn't speak.

What was there to say? He had won. After all her foolish resistance, after all her silly contracts and insults and pathetic attempts to appease him with half measures, he had broken past her defenses anyway.

He had forced her to do the one thing she'd sworn she'd never do.

Forced her? Even as she said it, she knew it wasn't true. She had wanted this. She'd been starving for this all her life. For him.

She turned her head away. She didn't want to meet his eyes, didn't want to see that lift of his eyebrow, the glimmer of triumph, maybe even the hint of disappointment that the victory had been a little too easy.

Too much like Missy Snowdon.

"Susannah," he said finally. She wondered if he might have been waiting for her to speak first, too.

"Sue, I'm sorry."

"No." She shut her eyes. "Don't say that. Don't say anything."

He lifted up onto one elbow. "Look, I know you didn't—"

"No," she said again. "Please, don't."

"We should talk."

Awkwardly, she stood. "No. It happened, that's all. *You win.* There's nothing else to say."

Trying not to imagine him watching her, she found her clothes and put them on. She couldn't do much, but she brushed a few crushed blades of grass out of her hair and wiped her hands on her grass-stained slacks.

And then, without so much as a backward glance, she left him.

SHE STAYED AT A HOTEL in Austin that night. She'd never run away from any challenge, any threat, any man, including her crazy grandfather. But she ran away from this.

She didn't run merely because she'd lost their battle. She didn't run because she'd revealed her physical need for him, which had survived eleven years of ice and anger.

She ran because, God help her, she had realized she was still in love with him.

She wondered if he knew that, too, just as he had known everything else.

She washed all traces of him away in the nameless hotel shower. But even when she was scrubbed clean on the outside, on the inside the love remained.

Wrapped in a scratchy white towel, she sat up on the bed all night, trying to talk herself out of it. Trying to make it not be true.

How could any passion be so powerful, so irrational, so impossible to annihilate? Paul's death hadn't destroyed this love. It hadn't died when Trent left her, or when he married someone else. His indifference, his sarcasm, his power trips...none of that had killed it.

If love survived all that, she was doomed. She'd carry the hopeless thing with her like a stone for the rest of her life. It would weigh her down, make her lonely, make her old. It would stand between her and any other love.

The night was long. But when dawn finally came, nothing had changed. She stood at the sealed window and looked down onto the city streets, aching, body and soul. She hadn't felt this frightened and lost since...

And then, with a fierce pang, she remembered.

Today was the anniversary of Paul's death.

CHAPTER THIRTEEN

SHE STAYED IN AUSTIN most of the morning. She bought a new dress on sale at a department store, tossed her grass-stained clothes into the bag the dress had come in, and dumped them in the trunk of her car. Then she did a dozen errands in a trance.

Because she'd already wasted the gas to get to Austin, she stopped by the corporate headquarters of SuperPantry, to find out whether they had reached a decision about her peaches. But she might as well have skipped it. The buyer apologized. They had already contracted for all the peaches they could move this year.

Susannah didn't even try to persuade him to change his mind. She didn't have the energy. Funny how everything was relative. Yesterday, the rejection would have felt like the end of the world. Today, it barely registered.

She called Nikki; she shopped for new hand tools; she checked out a new brand of peach bin. Eventually, though, she ran out of reasons to avoid going home.

Trent wasn't at Everly when she returned. Naturally, he would have to be at the Double C, which was his real job. He'd given Chase short shrift lately, focusing instead on helping out at Everly.

And, of course, he wouldn't really want to see her. Not for a while, anyhow.

Not till he needed another round of sex.

The house was quiet, still gleaming contentedly after the party preparations. She leafed through the mail, which was nothing but bills. She stared into the refrigerator, but nothing looked good. It was all peaches, in one form or another.

She decided to take another shower. She imagined she could still smell pine needles in her hair, and the musky odors of earth and rain, of hard work and sweat. Every time she took a breath, she remembered Trent moving inside her, and it was more than she could stand.

Climbing the stairs was torture, and she entered her bedroom slowly. It was as if all the strenuous, body-racking work of the past few weeks caught up with her at that very instant, and she could barely move without pain.

Her bed was still neatly made up, the white coverlet glowing in the sunlight that streamed in through the western window. She glanced at it, then stopped. Someone had left a piece of paper on her pillow.

Oddly, her first thought was of the graffiti scrawled on the walls of Trent's cottage. A chill tingled on her shoulder blades. Could this be some kind of hate mail, prompted by the anniversary of Paul's death?

But that was ridiculous, a specter summoned by her own guilty conscience, no doubt.

She picked up the paper. At the top was the printout of an e-mail Trent had received from someone named Catherine Overland at the Fresh Olive Markets in San Antonio, a company Susannah had never heard of.

Apparently, Catherine Overland would be delighted to talk to Ms. Everly about the peaches, if they were as good as Trent described. No, she had not yet signed any agreements for her new stores, and she could probably buy all Everly could provide.

She included a telephone number and said she'd wait to hear.

Susannah shook her head, disbelieving. She thought she'd come to the end of the road. She hadn't considered the possibility that Trent, too, was trying to work a miracle on her behalf.

And the thought that he might actually have succeeded...

She couldn't absorb it right away. The implications for Everly were just too big, and her mind was too tired.

She looked at the bottom of the page, where, below the e-mail, Trent had scrawled a few words in his spiky, decisive hand.

Let me know you're okay. Be careful today.

He'd signed it just *T.*

And then, below that, as if on impulse, he'd added these words.

No one wins, Sue. Not unless we talk.

She called Catherine Overland first. Even a prolonged business negotiation that would decide the future of her entire season sounded easier than calling Trent.

What would she say to him, anyhow? "Yes, I'm okay. And by the way, even though I still hate you for breaking my heart, I do appreciate your trying to save the orchard."

To her amazement, Catherine Overland took her call immediately. The owner of the Fresh Olive Markets sounded extremely interested in handling Everly's peaches. In fact, she was downright excited—they made an appointment to hammer out the details in person the very next day.

It seemed almost like one of her dreams. Susannah tried to remain cautious, but in spite of her best efforts she felt a shimmer of hope. Was it possible that the long, anxious struggle had really come to an end?

For several minutes, she sat on the edge of her bed, with the sunshine warming her back, and stared at her cell phone, squeezing it as if to convince herself it was real.

She had to call him. She had to thank him, although she wondered if she could find the words to thank someone for dropping a miracle in her lap. Maybe she should send him an e-mail….

No. That was the coward's way out. Besides, if he felt edgy about the anniversary date, especially after the vandalism at his house, she should let him know she was all right. She couldn't keep putting it off.

Slowly, she punched in the number for his office at the Double C. She held her breath, but luck was on her side. It went to the machine after several rings. He must be out on the property.

"This is Trent. I'm not available right now…"

He sounded so businesslike. That helped, but even so, the sound of his voice slid into her and stirred something deep in her midsection.

"Hi," she said after the beep. "I just wanted you to know I got your note. I just talked to Catherine Overland, and it looks quite promising. Thank you very much for setting that up."

It sounded stiff, and the level of gratitude was obviously not proportional to the service rendered. She hesitated and then tried again. "Really, it is a wonderful development. Thanks a lot."

Should she mention his postscript? She couldn't imagine what she'd say, so she just hung up.

She took her shower, then, about twice as long as usual and as hot as she could bear. When she got out, she wrapped herself in her white terry robe, put her hair in a towel, and wondered whether she could just climb into bed, wet hair and all, and sleep away this strange, unsettling day.

But from her bedroom window she could see the front driveway. And Chase's truck was out there.

He must have been knocking while she was in the shower, because she heard the sound of the front door opening. He must be anxious, because he never used his copy of the key.

"Susannah? Susannah?"

He started taking the stairs two by two, just as she came hurrying down to greet him. They nearly collided on the landing.

"Damn it, there you are!" He took her by the shoulders, obviously frustrated. "For God's sake, give a man a heart attack, why don't you? Your car's out there, but you don't answer the door, you don't answer the phone..."

She put her hand on his chest to slow him down. "For heaven's sake. Do I have to check in with you when I take a shower now?"

"Today you do. You haven't forgotten what day it is, have you?"

"Of course not." She tied the belt of her terry robe tighter. "But why is everyone so uptight about that this year? Is it because of what happened to Trent's cottage?"

Chase scowled. It was such a rare expression to see on his sunny face that something inside her fluttered nervously.

"What's going on?" She remembered, abruptly, the tension in Trent's posture when she'd showed up in the woods last night. Almost as if he'd been on guard, waiting for trouble.

"What?" She jiggled her hands against Chase's chest. "Tell me. Has there been something else, too?"

"He didn't tell you?"

"I guess not. Damn it, Chase. *What?*"

He hesitated. "Maybe he didn't want to…" He glanced up the stairs. "I don't see his car out front. Has he been here and gone already?"

"No. I thought he was at the Double C." The flutter inside intensified. "Isn't he working with you today?"

"He was. About an hour ago, though, he said he was going to come back here, to see if you'd shown up. That was a pretty stupid stunt you pulled last night, actually. Taking off without letting anyone know where you were going."

She saw that now, but she couldn't turn back the clock. "I know. It's just that he…that we—" She tried to read Chase's face. But it looked so stern. "Did he tell you what happened last night?"

"No details. He just said that you were mad as hell, and that he'd pretty royally screwed things up."

"Did he tell you about Missy Snowdon?"

Chase grimaced. "He didn't have to tell me. I was there. Man, you should see that woman, Sue. It's creepy, and kind of sad, actually. She used to be smoking hot." He held up his hands. "Sorry, I know you hated her, but she was hot."

Susannah didn't bother to dispute that. She was still hung up on the first part of his answer. "What do you mean, you were there?"

"I mean, I was *there*. When Missy showed up at his office, all drunk and blubbering, he sent an SOS by way of Josie. I came flying over to do an emergency blood-sucking-stalker extraction."

He chuckled, clearly amused by something in the memory. But then his face sobered again. "Wait a minute. You weren't thinking that…"

She took a breath and lifted her chin.

Chase groaned. "Oh, God*damn* it, Sue. Is that what this fight between you two is all about? Are you out of your mind? *Missy Snowdon?*"

"Well, it wouldn't be the first time, would it?" She fought the rising anxiety that told her she'd been a fool, and done something truly stupid.

"Trent kissed her, Chase. Nell Bollinger saw them, and she called me, because she thought I ought to know."

"Nell Bollinger is a Puritan busybody. If there was any kissing going on, it was Missy kissing Trent, not the other way around. She was drunk, and desperate, and—"

He ran his hand through his hair, obviously exasperated beyond his power to express.

"And frankly, Sue, you should know by now that Trent just isn't a cheater. Yeah, yeah, I know he did it before. But you really need to let go of that crap from eleven years ago, sweetheart. None of us are the same people we were then."

"I—"

"No, not even you, Sue. Especially you. Trent is a man now, not a boy. He was immature back then, and maybe he was insecure. He isn't either one of those things anymore. You need to wake up and see who you're really married to. Before it's too late."

She looked at Chase's face, misery swarming through her. He had been her friend longer than anyone, longer even than Trent. He had never lied to her.

She wanted to believe him.

In fact, she suddenly realized that she *did* believe him.

She didn't really think that Trent was a liar or a cheater. She thought he was a smart, gorgeous, loyal and highly sexual man. Though she would never have admitted it, she had chosen him for a temporary husband because she believed that he, of all men, could be trusted to treat her fairly.

And she'd chosen him because, deep inside, she still loved him, still wanted him, still longed to be his wife…even if just for a little while.

Why hadn't she been willing to see all this before? The person she didn't trust was herself.

She didn't trust that she could be woman enough for a man like Trent.

She expected him to cheat today for the same reason

she'd expected him to cheat back then. Because she had no faith in her ability to keep him satisfied.

And blaming him was less painful than blaming herself.

She pulled the towel off her hair, and let it all cascade, wet and snarled, around her shoulders. Someday she would admit all this to Chase and, she prayed, to Trent. But right now there wasn't time.

"Chase, did you say he left an hour ago?"

He nodded. He pulled out his cell and punched one of his speed dials. He listened quite a while, and then he spoke. "Trent, give me a call, okay? Sue's fine. It's you we're worried about now, so let me know where you are, okay?"

When he hung up, Susannah's heart was pounding. "He's not answering?"

"No. That doesn't feel right, because he always answers when he's working. It could be something urgent. It could be one of the horses. Damn it." He beat the phone against his palm. "Can you think of anywhere else he might have gone?"

"He doesn't tell me much. He sometimes is gone on the weekends, but I have no idea where—"

"Oh, that's Peggy. Almost every weekend he helps her with stuff around the house. But I don't think that today of all days—"

"Peggy? Peggy Archer?" Could this be Trent they were discussing? She felt as if she were talking about a man she'd never even met. "What do you mean, he helps Peggy?"

Chase tilted his head, as if he couldn't believe what

he was hearing. His eyes narrowed, their expression judging her and finding her unworthy. It hurt more than she could have imagined.

"You don't ever even talk to him, do you, Sue? No wonder you don't understand what kind of man he is."

He put his phone back in his pocket and turned to go down the stairs. At the bottom, he looked back up at her.

"He left us once before, because you refused to forgive him. I know it was hard for you, but did you ever think that it was hard for the rest of us, too? We loved him, too. And we lost him for years. And now… Damn it, Sue. If you've driven him off again…"

He didn't finish the sentence. He didn't need to.

She nodded slowly, acknowledging all of it. The weight of it felt heavy on her heart.

"We'll find him," she said. "And if you get to him before I do, will you give him a message for me?"

"What?"

"Tell him I'm ready to talk."

THE HALF AN HOUR it took Susannah to drive to Peggy Archer's house in Darlonsville seemed endless. She kept her phone on her lap, and alternated calling Peggy's house and Trent's cell, over and over and over.

But each time the calls were answered by machines.

She heard once from Chase, and the news wasn't great. He'd been everywhere he could think of, including Paul's cemetery plot, and turned up nothing. Trent still hadn't returned his call.

When she finally parked on the street in front of the

small white house with the blue door, she let the engine idle while she double-checked the address.

She'd never seen Peggy's new home before, and this looked awfully modest for a woman who used to preside over a ten-thousand-acre ranch with a five-thousand square-foot main house.

Hadn't Peggy received anything in her divorce settlement?

Susannah was just stalling. Of course this was Peggy's house. A gold Honda sat in the carport—and if it weren't Peggy's that would have been a coincidence too huge to swallow.

The truth was she just didn't want to face the woman again. But if there was any chance Peggy knew where Trent might be...

Susannah killed the engine, went up to the small front porch and knocked on the blue door.

It took so long that Susannah wondered whether Peggy might simply have decided not to open it. Or maybe, since she hadn't answered her phone, either, she really wasn't home. Maybe she was out with a friend, in another car.

Susannah's heart beat a little faster. She wasn't sure where to go next.

But then the door opened and Peggy stood there, holding a light sweater closed with one fist. She looked exhausted. Her red, wavy hair needed cutting, and brushing wouldn't have hurt, either. Her eyes looked sunken in swollen red-rimmed sockets.

On the other hand, Susannah knew she didn't look all that great herself. She had come out with wet hair and no makeup, wearing the first pair of jeans and T-shirt she could grab.

"Mrs. Archer. I'm sorry to bother you, but I wondered if you might have spoken to Trent today."

Peggy stared at Susannah, not answering. It probably lasted only two or three seconds, but it was extremely uncomfortable. Susannah had the feeling she was being judged, down to her socks and her soul.

"Trent always calls me on Paul's anniversary." Peggy blinked slowly, and Susannah wondered whether she might have been popping those pain pills again. "Always. First thing in the morning."

Which was more, her tone implied, than Susannah had ever done. And Susannah couldn't deny it. It felt strange to face the fact that, though she had always accused Trent of running away from the tragedy, she was the one who really had done so.

She might have stayed in Eastcreek physically, but emotionally she had retreated into the cold fortress she'd created inside herself. She had shared her feelings with no one, mourning Paul only in private.

But Trent had found the courage to reach out, open up…expose himself to the pain.

Susannah nodded. "But you haven't heard from him since then?"

"No. Now, if you'll excuse me…"

Susannah put out her hand to keep the door from falling shut. "Mrs. Archer, please. I'm worried about him. We don't know where he is, and he doesn't answer his telephone."

The corner of the older woman's mouth rose. "Maybe he just doesn't want to talk to you."

Susannah wondered how much Trent had told this woman about their marriage. Her cheeks felt hot, as she realized that there was very little he could have said that was even remotely flattering.

"That's possible," she admitted. "But he isn't answering Chase's calls, either. And there have been some strange things happening. I'm just…worried."

Peggy's expression sharpened. "What kind of things?"

"Nothing big, really, nothing that couldn't be explained away, I guess. He had an accident when he was working at Everly—a broken ladder. That might have been nothing, but a couple of days ago someone spray painted the word *murderer* on his house. And Chase told me that yesterday morning, Trent found a copperhead in his office."

She felt her heart begin to thump as she enumerated the episodes. Together, they sounded more sinister. And if she had known about the snake, she would have run to him instantly. Maybe she could have stopped him from…

From doing whatever he'd done. From going wherever he'd gone.

Or from falling into whatever trap had been laid for him.

"Maybe it's just coincidence, but you can see how strange it seems—"

"Oh, God." Peggy staggered slightly but managed to use the door for balance. "Oh, God, I was afraid of this."

Susannah frowned. "Of what?"

The older woman stepped away from the door.

"Come in, Susannah," she said. "We need to make a telephone call."

Susannah followed numbly as Peggy limped through a neat, elegantly decorated living room, all the way to a tidy blue kitchen. She picked up a cordless phone and began to enter numbers rapidly.

"Who are you calling?" Susannah tried to see the numbers, but the older woman's fingers were flying too fast. "Do you know where he is?"

"I hope not," Peggy said cryptically.

She got no answer at the first number, so she tried a second. And then, with a muffled oath, a third.

And then she started slightly, as if she hadn't really expected this number to get an answer. "Nora? It's Peggy. I need to talk to Harrison."

Susannah put her hands on the countertop. The cool granite soothed her hot fingers.

"Damn it." Peggy's jaw tightened. "Where is he? Exactly?"

She made a frustrated noise. "Well, how long has he been gone? I need to know, Nora. It's important. Why? Because this is the anniversary of Paul's death, and he's been acting crazy. I'm afraid he might be about to do something stupid."

For a long time, Peggy just listened. As the seconds stretched on, Susannah felt herself growing more anxious than ever. What did Peggy know about Harrison that made her so sure this was the call they needed to make? And what was she hearing now, that made her already-exhausted face seem to crumble down to dust?

"Peggy, what is it?" Susannah couldn't just sit quietly. She took the woman's arm, which seemed to be trembling.

"Oh, my God," Peggy breathed into the phone. "Nora, I'm so sorry."

More listening. Susannah didn't let go of the older woman's arm. Tears had begun to stream down Peggy's face, though she wasn't making any sobbing noises. She wasn't making any sounds at all. Susannah couldn't even hear her breathing.

"All right, Nora, look. Here's what I want you to do. Call Harrison's cell. Don't stop calling it, even if he doesn't answer. It might help him just to remember you're still out there."

Susannah began to breathe lightly and rapidly through her mouth. She noticed a blue-and-white-checked porcelain rooster on one of the corner shelves. She remembered that rooster, from the years when she used to play at Paul's ranch. It was the only thing in this house that seemed at all familiar.

Once, when they were about ten, Paul had taken one of his father's rifles and pointed it at the rooster, pretending to shoot it. The memory sent a shiver through Susannah's torso, and for a minute she couldn't figure out why.

Then she understood. It wasn't the rooster that scared her. It was the rifle.

"No, Nora, I'm not sure where he is. I don't have anything more than a hunch." Peggy wiped her brow with a trembling hand, but she kept her voice admirably steady, as if she didn't want to alarm the other woman further.

"I think it's just barely possible he went to the pool. No, you don't know it, it's just a place where he and Paul used to fish. No, I don't want you to go there. If you're at your mother's house you're too far away anyhow. You keep calling him. Susannah and I will go to the pool."

Susannah grabbed her purse and began digging out the keys. Her hands were shaking, too.

The rest of Peggy's conversation was a blur to her. Her feet were tingling, as if they couldn't bear standing still, as if they needed to run. She held the keys so tightly the metal grew warm in her palm.

Finally, Peggy hung up. She turned to Susannah. Her face was all tears and ashen strain.

"What is it? Peggy, what happened? Why are you crying?"

"Harrison is dying," she said, the simplicity of the words sharpening their impact. "Nora says he has pancreatic cancer. They can't stop it. They told him he has only a few weeks to live. He won't..."

Her voice broke slightly for the first time. "He won't make it to Paul's next anniversary."

Susannah tried to absorb the information.

"I'm sorry, Peggy," she said, well aware that her condolences would mean little. She wasn't even sure why Peggy cared so very much, since Harrison had always been a difficult man, even when he was her husband. He hadn't been a real part of Peggy's life for almost ten years.

She didn't want to be insensitive, but she was confused. Was this merely heartbreaking personal news that had erased everything else from Peggy's heart?

Or was it somehow tied to Trent?

"We need to go to Green Fern Pool," Peggy said. She glanced around, her eyes still streaming with tears. "I don't know where my purse is."

"I'll drive." Susannah put her hand on the older woman's arm again. "Help me to understand, Peggy. The fact that Harrison is sick…does that have anything to do with Trent?"

Peggy looked at her through those dazed, flooded eyes. "Of course it does," she said. "Surely you knew he always wanted to make Trent pay for Paul's death. He always said that someday he'd get revenge."

No, Susannah had not known that. She had, in fact, believed that Harrison had recovered nicely. That his heart was now totally invested in his new family.

But then she remembered his gray face when he'd shown up at the peach party. His stiff posture that had said he almost couldn't force himself to stay…

"But even if he wanted to hurt Trent…why now, after all these years? Why today?"

Peggy shook her head. "Can't you see? This is the day Harrison has been waiting for."

"What day?"

"The day he has nothing to live for. The day he has nothing to lose."

CHAPTER FOURTEEN

GREEN FERN POOL was so well hidden that, although it was probably the most beautiful spot in Eastcreek, it was practically a secret, even from the locals.

Technically, it was on Double C land, but so far out on the extreme edges of the property that it felt like another world.

Geographically, it was just a wrinkle in the meandering path of Clayton Creek. Right there, the creek followed the contours of the land into a small ravine, bubbled out into a fifteen-foot-deep swimming hole, then narrowed up again and burbled into the next county in its usual lazy way.

You couldn't get to it by car. The Fugitive Four used to walk from Chase's house, mostly, but that was the long way. Today, not knowing whether every second counted, Susannah couldn't risk it. She pulled her car onto the shoulder of the closest county road, very near where she'd changed Peggy's tire.

She turned to the older woman now. "That day, when you said you were following me—"

"I was following Harrison," Peggy said simply. "He scared me. I knew something was wrong. And he had been following you."

That had happened at least a week ago. And Peggy hadn't warned anyone? "You've known that long?"

"I haven't *known*." Peggy shut her eyes and shook her head wearily. "I still don't *know*. I have no proof. All I have is fear. I wanted to be wrong."

Susannah understood that all too well. On the way here, they'd both been trying to persuade themselves that the fear was unfounded, that Trent was simply angry and looking for some time alone.

Susannah had phoned Chase, but the call had gone immediately to voice mail, as if he were on the other line. She left a message, just the bare bones information that Harrison was gravely ill, and that Susannah and Peggy were going to take a quick look at Green Fern Pool.

She was sure he could fill in the blanks. If he hadn't found Trent yet, he'd probably join them here within a very few minutes.

If he *had* found Trent, maybe they'd all meet here. She hoped that they'd have a good laugh, teasing Susannah and Peggy for allowing the situation to become so melodramatic.

She tried to visualize the day arriving at that happy ending. She tried to make it come true just by believing in it with all her heart.

The land tilted toward the ravine here, so she put on the manual brake and the hazard lights.

Then she turned again to Peggy. "I can get there faster if I go on ahead. You can come at your own pace. Do you mind?"

"No. I understand. My leg's so bad, I'd stay here, but…" She looked out the window, as if she might be able to see all the way down to the swimming hole, though the only view was of deep green oaks and silvery pines.

"I should come," she said. "If they are there, I might be able to get through to Harrison. I'm the only one who really knows what this day can do to you."

The sadness in her voice touched Susannah. "Maybe they won't be there," she said, as they'd each said a dozen times on this trip.

"Go." Peggy put her hand on Susannah's arm. "Maybe it's not too late. Harrison doesn't really want to hurt anyone, you know. He just wants his own pain to stop."

Susannah nodded, got out of the car and quickly walked back to where the head of the sandy path fed out onto the road. She was glad her tennis shoes had been closest to hand when she got dressed. If flip-flops or stilettos had been nearby, she would have chosen them, and then this twisting path would have spelled disaster.

Even with sneakers for traction, she held on to branches as she made her way down. The vegetation formed a thick wall around the hole, so she couldn't see anything that mattered.

She tried to be quiet, but, as she drew near the black gum trees that formed Heaven's Gate, she slipped, making a terrible racket as pebbles skidded away from her shoes.

"Don't come here," a man's voice called out angrily. "Whoever you are, stay away."

For a moment, Susannah's heart stopped. The voice was thick, altered by emotion, but she was almost certain it belonged to Harrison Archer.

She didn't let herself think it over. She simply ducked between the branches, dashed through the few yards of growth that sheltered the hole and emerged, breathless, on the other side.

It was like walking right into a nightmare. Before her lay the exact scenario she'd been playing in her head all the way from Darlonsville.

Just about twenty feet in front of her, Trent stood on the boat launch rock, with his back to the water. The crisscrossing shafts of sunlight spotlighted him, as if this was a theatrical performance, and he was the star.

Harrison Archer was planted, legs spread for balance, a few feet above them both, on the low edge of the southern limestone wall.

A patch of wild red phlox grew at his feet. He appeared to be standing in a pool of blood.

He had a long, black rifle in his hands. It was pointed at Trent.

"Sue, get out of here," Trent said, his voice calm. He turned his head halfway, so he could look at her while still keeping Harrison in his peripheral vision. "He won't try to stop you. Just go."

"The hell I won't." Harrison stared at Susannah, though the rifle remained trained on Trent. "Stay exactly where you are."

Susannah didn't let herself move. Everyone in Eastcreek knew that Harrison Archer was a lifelong hunter, a stalker with nerves of steel. He held all the local records for marksmanship.

She'd made a mistake by coming in here, but it was too late to change that now. If this man decided that

Trent or Susannah, or both, would die here today, then they were probably going to die.

And yet, somehow, it didn't seem possible that this was really happening. It was such a beautiful day, and the blue water sparkled beside them, as if it were encrusted with diamonds. The trees waved gently in the balmy air, and somewhere not far away a tree swallow was twittering.

As if answering the bird's song, a cell phone suddenly started to ring. She glanced at Trent, who shook his head.

"In the pool," he said softly. She understood. Harrison had thrown—or made Trent throw—his cell phone into the water.

Which meant that it was Harrison's cell ringing.

Nora, following Peggy's instructions.

Though Harrison didn't answer it, the noise seemed to hold his attention. Susannah prayed that Peggy had been right. Maybe this reminder of the outside world, and the living, breathing people who had just as much claim on his heart as Paul did, might prevent him from pulling that trigger.

When the ringing stopped, Harrison's gaze swung back to Trent. They might have been continuing a casual conversation.

"Do you know what I talked about, the last time I saw Paul? *You.* Isn't that ironic? We were right there, where you're standing now, and I asked him why he couldn't get better grades. Like you."

He made a low, growling sound, like an animal in pain. "The last time I was ever going to see my boy whole, and I told him I wanted him to be more like *you.*"

The cell phone began to ring again. He touched his pocket, either to smother the noise or to tenderly connect with the source. It was impossible to tell which.

When the ringing stopped, the man started to sob openly.

"Get out of here, Sue." Trent's voice was calm but insistent. "Right now. Just go."

She looked at him. She was terrified, but not of being shot. "I'm not going to leave you," she said.

"Shut up," Harrison barked, shaking his head. He breathed heavily and let out a tortured sob. "This isn't about the two of you. This is about Paul. My boy. My boy died believing that I thought you were a better man."

"He didn't think that, Harrison." Trent sounded reasonable and completely unafraid. "He knew you loved him. And he loved you, too."

But Harrison didn't seem to hear him. The cell phone had begun again and he just kept shaking his head, as if to flick away the noise that fractured his concentration.

He seemed to be struggling to hold on to a train of thought. "I damn sure don't think you're the better man now, Maxwell. I think you're a murderer. You don't deserve any of the happiness you've had. You don't deserve anything. This bullet's too good for you. You ought to have to suffer, the way my boy did."

The disjointed sentences showed a mental state even more disturbing than Susannah had imagined. It was unlikely that pure logic would hold much sway over this tormented mind.

She remembered the months Paul's parents had kept a vigil by his bedside, knowing he couldn't recover from his burns but unwilling to turn off the machines that kept the body breathing. She had wondered then how any parent could survive the experience with sense and soul intact.

She knew now that they couldn't. Harrison's broken heart had broken his mind, as well.

"Mr. Archer," she said impulsively. "Paul's death really wasn't Trent's fault. It was mine. I'm the one who caused the whole terrible thing."

"Susannah." Trent's body seemed coiled with tension. "Be quiet."

"It's true." She kept going, hoping that, at the very least, she could buy enough time for Peggy to call the police. Surely by now the older woman had come close enough to understand the situation.

Peggy was smart—smarter than Susannah. She wouldn't join them, giving Harrison one more sitting duck to pick off. She'd climb back up to the car and telephone for help.

If only she didn't move so slowly...

"Trent had done something to hurt me, and I wanted to get even. I asked Paul to help me make Trent mad. I asked him to flirt with me, to dance with me."

She wasn't sure whether this might backfire. Her facts were correct, but her logic was faulty. She had set the tragedy in motion, yes, but it had been Trent's fist that slammed into Paul's face, knocking him over the table, causing the kerosene lamp to ignite the hay.

Ironically, Paul's face had been the only part of him

untouched by the flames, so that Trent's damage was easily identified. The broken nose, the blackened eye…such little problems compared to the burns.

But his parents had kissed that bruised face every day, praying for a miracle that didn't come.

Could a father ever forget who had done that to his son?

Harrison still wept, but he seemed to be listening, which meant he wasn't shooting. So she kept talking.

"It was all my fault," she said. "It was such a stupid way to deal with my pain. If I'd had the courage to just go to Trent and talk to him, instead of using Paul—"

"Yes, you did. You *used* him." As if the information had just sunk in, Harrison moved the rifle's barrel. He stared at Susannah now, and for the first time aimed his weapon at her. "You bitch. You used him, and you killed him."

"She's lying." Trent's voice was suddenly as loud, as authoritative as Harrison's. He made a small move, just enough to startle the older man, causing him to swing the barrel back in Trent's direction. "She had no part in it. The fight was between me and Paul. No one else."

"Shut up, both of you." Harrison's cell began to ring again, and he looked as if he might explode from all the mixed signals. "Do you think I care which one of you killed him? He's dead. He's *dead*."

Miraculously, his mind seemed to clear. And his focus returned.

He lifted the rifle, tilting it so that he peered down the barrel, which pointed straight at Trent's heart. He looked like the consummate hunter he was.

Susannah started to shift her feet. She had to do something, even though it was obviously hopeless. Maybe she'd die for Trent, and maybe she'd die with him. But either one would be better than living without him.

Before her brain could send the signal to her legs, the sound of running feet broke the terrible green silence.

A boy's voice cried out frantically.

"Dad!"

Finally, Harrison lost his focus. The barrel of the gun dropped, and he looked around wildly, as if a ghost had called to him.

"Dad!"

Susannah and Trent turned simultaneously, and she knew that, for both of them, it was a heart-stopping moment. A little red-haired boy, maybe eight years old, the spitting image of Paul Archer, came slipping and skidding down the slanted, mossy walls of the swimming hole, barreling toward his father.

"Dad, don't!"

Behind him, Nora Archer was running, too, her younger son clasped firmly by the hand. A few yards behind the frightened family, Peggy limped toward them.

Susannah looked up at the man on the wall. For a moment she feared the others had come too late. Harrison seemed too far gone, too committed to his plan, to let anything, even the horror on his son's innocent face, stop him from exacting his revenge.

"Go home, Sean." Harrison's voice was so choked with tears the words were almost in another language. "You don't understand. This man…he killed my son."

The little boy froze in place, just ten feet away from Trent. He stared at his father, his mouth working, his eyes filling with tears.

Finally he spoke, his high-pitched voice clear in the quiet air.

"But what about us, Dad? We're your sons, too."

Harrison looked down at the boy, whose red hair gleamed like copper in the sunlight. Under the freckles, the small face was white with terror.

The man made a strangled sound, as he faced the impossible dilemma of choosing between the child he'd lost so long ago and the one who stood before him now.

"Sean," he said.

The one word carried the sound of ultimate defeat.

A warm gust of wind penetrated the trees. When it kissed Susannah's cheeks, she realized they were streaming with tears.

And then, as sirens began to wail in the distance, Harrison bowed his head. The rifle fell awkwardly from his limp fingers. It clattered over the edge of the limestone wall, slid down a shaft of sunlight and sank without a splash into the pool below.

CHAPTER FIFTEEN

UNTANGLING the tragic story at the sheriff's office took hours, even though Trent thought it should have been fairly easy.

Harrison openly admitted everything. He explained that he'd hired Eli Breslin to vandalize the cottage, but when Trent fired the boy, Harrison had been forced to deposit the copperhead in Trent's office himself.

By then, of course, he'd been given the news that he had only a few weeks to live anyhow. So the risk of handling the poisonous snake hadn't bothered him at all.

The ladder...well, that was just a rotten ladder. But Trent's suspicion of something more sinister had probably been his subconscious trying to tell him to beware.

The police wanted to know whether Harrison had wanted to kill Trent. Harrison answered that one slowly. He'd thought he did. But from a distance the concept of killing seemed easier.

When he had found himself face-to-face with his victim, it hadn't been quite that simple. He hadn't been able to make himself pull the trigger.

Peggy had been horrified to find that Harrison had

tried to divert suspicion to her. And he'd succeeded. He'd lured Trent to Green Fern Pool by pretending that Peggy had Susannah cornered there. Primed by Harrison's earlier comments, Trent had swallowed the bait instantly.

The deputies went over everything a dozen times. Trent remembered this strategy from the night of the fire. No matter how cut-and-dried a situation seemed, the authorities liked to cross every T, then come back and cross it again through another witness's official statement.

All the people involved—Trent, Susannah, Harrison, Peggy and Nora—were interviewed separately. Only Sean, who seemed to have aged ten years in that one afternoon, was allowed the moral support of another person, and clung to his mom like glue.

Perhaps the police were just being diligent, but around midnight, when Trent passed Susannah in the hall and saw the exhausted circles under her eyes, he decided enough was enough.

He was going to take her home. If the deputies wanted another statement, they could get it in the morning.

They left her car at the station, and Trent did the driving. Good thing he did. About halfway there, she fell asleep.

As Trent pulled into Everly's drive, he saw warm, welcoming lights burning everywhere. Chase and Josie must have stopped by, aware that, after such a harrowing day, it would be grim to return to a cold, dark house.

He sent a mental thanks to the newlyweds.

He didn't get out of the car right away. He hated to wake Susannah, and he was tired, too. The climb to the porch seemed like scaling Mt. Everest. So he reclined his seat and watched the stars bob silently in the liquid midnight sky.

After a few minutes, Susannah stirred. She made that small purring hum that had always signaled the end of a catnap.

She opened her eyes. "Are we home?"

His chest tightened. He realized that, though he couldn't pinpoint the moment, he had begun to think of Everly as home.

But was that a mistake? They hadn't had a minute alone since the police had arrived at the pool. They hadn't exchanged a single private word. He had no idea how she felt. About him. About them. About anything.

When she'd stood beside him out at the swimming hole, refusing to leave in spite of the danger, he had thought that perhaps…

But at that moment, all emotions had been artificially heightened. It was as if, while they were facing death, hidden in that eerie green nook, they had been under a temporary enchantment. A spell woven of fear and danger.

The spell was broken now. They were back in reality. And the rules were different here.

"Yeah, we're home. I was just enjoying the night. It's nice, lots of stars." He smiled. "Looks like one of Nikki's kindergarten art projects."

Susannah shifted so that she could see the sky, as well. "Yeah," she agreed, trying to smile while she stifled a yawn. "Nikki always did have a heavy hand with the glitter."

He touched her shoulder. "Come on. You're exhausted. Let's go in."

She nodded and yawned again. "Still," she said with a smile, "I'm pretty sure it's better to be exhausted than dead."

He laughed, more because he loved her spunk than because the joke was particularly funny.

It had been terrifying, watching Harrison swivel the rifle toward Susannah. Trent had already been out there, facing that same weapon, for at least fifteen minutes before Susannah arrived. But that was the first moment he had felt true fear.

He had been fairly sure that, as long as nothing spooked the man, Harrison would never work up the courage to fire. Killing Trent wouldn't bring Paul back, and somewhere in his gut Harrison knew that.

But "fairly sure" wasn't enough, not when it was Susannah the man had in his sights.

"You were amazing," he said. He wanted to reach over and scoop her into his arms, but he didn't. "I might be dead if you hadn't arrived when you did. You may well be the gutsiest woman I've ever met."

"Are you kidding? I was scared to death. You know that woodpecker you thought you heard? That was actually my knees knocking."

"Oh." He chuckled. "I thought it was mine."

She took a deep breath that turned into another yawn.

"Trent." She turned to him with a somber gaze. "Do you think he would really have done it? If Sean and Nora hadn't showed up when they did?"

"I don't know," he answered honestly. "I was telling

myself he wouldn't. But when I made my calculations, I didn't know about the cancer. That could have changed everything."

They were silent a moment, and he knew they were thinking the same thing. Everything could have ended today. But it hadn't. They still had lives to live.

And decisions to make.

"Come on," he said again. This time she got out of the car without demur. They made their way up the porch steps slowly. He stood back and let her unlock the door.

"Are you hungry?" Trent glanced toward the kitchen.

Susannah shook her head. "I should be, but I guess I ate too many of those horrible crackers at the station. I think I just want to go to bed."

"Okay," he said, trying to sound as neutral as possible. He obviously wasn't going to put any pressure on her tonight, and he hoped she knew that.

A good night's sleep, and a little distance from the nightmare of today, might improve his chances anyhow. Right now, she was exhausted, drained.

Or so he told himself. But the truth was simpler. He didn't want to ask her how she felt, because he was afraid she might tell him she felt nothing.

She waited at the foot of the stairs while he circled the first floor, turning off all the lights Josie and Chase had left burning. He checked the doors and windows, too, just in case Susannah still felt a little nervous.

Of course, they both knew the danger was over. Harrison had been checked into the hospital for a psychiatric evaluation. Trent's bet was that the poor guy would go straight from there to the medical wing, and from there to his final resting place beside his firstborn son.

But he didn't want Susannah's sleep haunted by dreams of snakes and rifles and pain-mad men who cried "murder" in the night. If she dreamed at all, he selfishly wanted her to dream of him.

He joined her where she waited, and the two of them quietly climbed the stairs together.

Her bedroom was at the top of the staircase, and the door was standing open. The four-poster bed beyond was turned down, the night-light gleaming, casting honeyed shadows on the sheets.

He knew he had to let her go. But damn it. How was he supposed to find the strength to walk away?

He loved her. That's where his strength had to come from. He loved her enough to let her decide, without any pressure.

He'd tried to fight his way into her heart, and he'd tried to seduce his way in. Neither had worked.

Maybe it was time to stop trying. Maybe it was time to leave her in peace.

He tightened his resolve.

"Good night, Sue," he said. He touched her cheek with a knuckle, knowing that if he allowed any more contact than that, he'd be sunk. "Thank you for saving me today."

She looked embarrassed. "I didn't—"

"Yes." He put his finger across her lips. "You did."

She smiled, and he let his hand fall rather than feel the soft warmth of her mouth move against his skin.

"Well, if I did, it's only fair," she said softly. "You've saved me, and Everly, too."

Oh, hell, he had to get out of here. He was so tired he could hardly remember his name, and yet he wanted to take her into that room, lay her onto those soft white sheets, and make love to her until the stars went out in a blaze of dawn.

"Good. I'm glad." His voice sounded as if it came from a wooden puppet. But it was difficult to force the polite phrases out when all he wanted to say was, *Please forgive me, Sue. I love you.*

He turned, looking at the long hall that led to his own room. The one that had once belonged to her grandfather. She would never come to him there.

"Trent—"

Her hand reached out and gently wrapped around his forearm. Her fingers were tanned, from the hard orchard work she did every day of her life. And yet they were cool and smooth and graceful. He remembered how they had felt as they stroked him.

"What is it, Sue?"

"I was hoping… You see, I don't really want to be alone tonight."

Instinctively, his body reacted. Heat gathered in his loins.

"What do you mean?" He looked back at her. "I don't want to misunderstand. What exactly are you asking?"

She tilted her head and her hair, so sensual in its unstyled freedom, glowed under the hall light. "I'd like you to stay with me tonight, but…"

"But?"

Her eyes were serious. "I have a document I'd like you to sign. I wrote it while we were waiting at the station."

Something painful stabbed through his heart.

"Something to sign?" He almost laughed, except that it hurt too much.

He shook his head, defeated. "I can't do this anymore. I can't wait around, dying inside, while you try to decide how much punishment is enough. I love you, Susannah. But if we can't let the past go now, after everything that's happened, then we really do have no future."

He moved, but she wouldn't let go of his arm.

"Please," she said, digging in her pocket. "Read it."

She pulled out a scrap of paper, and searched his face with her earnest gaze. He wondered if his expression looked as hard and discouraged as he felt.

"Please, Trent."

He nodded numbly and took the paper she was holding out.

She must have found it on one of the desks at the station. It was a torn piece from a pink While You Were Out pad.

He unfolded it and began to read.

I, Trent Maxwell, promise that I will love and cherish my wife forever,

He looked up at her, wondering if this was a joke, some new torture…

She raised her eyebrows. "There's more," she said. "Go on."

Because, even though she's been proud and judgmental and—

He had to turn the paper sideways, as Susannah had run out of room.

—and kind of a bitch…

He turned the paper again. His heart was suddenly lighter, pumping hard again in his chest.

…she loves me very much.

He stared at the paper, afraid to move for fear the words would swim away, a mirage all along.

Could it possibly be true? Could her love have survived the anger, buried somewhere under the resentment and pain? After all these years, could forgiveness have finally arrived?

He looked up again. "Sue—"

"No," she said firmly. "You're just getting to the important part."

He turned over the paper, and found one last scrawl.

PS—I also promise to refer all future visits from that nasty tramp Missy Snowdon to aforementioned wife, who will kick her pretty little—

"I ran out of paper." Susannah smiled. "But I'm sure you get the idea."

"Yes." Trent could barely think, his heart was beating so fast. He looked at his brave, beautiful, stubborn wife and tried to believe this moment had finally come. "I'm…well, I'm getting quite a few ideas, actually."

"Excellent," she said with a satisfied sigh. She patted his chest with her fingers. "But I do think we need to hurry, Trent, because I wouldn't want to fall asleep right in the middle of one of them."

"Oh, no, Mrs. Maxwell." He laughed for joy as he scooped her into his arms. "We have almost eleven years to make up for. I can guarantee—in writing if you like—that no one will sleep in Everly tonight."

* * * * *

*Celebrate 60 years of pure
reading pleasure with Harlequin!*

To commemorate the event, Harlequin Intrigue®
is thrilled to invite you to the wedding of The Colby
Agency's J. T. Baxley and his bride, Eve Mattson.

That is, of course, if J.T. can find the woman who
left him at the altar. Considering he's a private in-
vestigator for one of the top agencies in the
country—the best of the best—that shouldn't be
a problem. The real setback is that his bride isn't
who she appears to be…and her mysterious past
has put them both in danger.

*Enjoy an exclusive glimpse of
Debra Webb's latest addition to*
THE COLBY AGENCY: ELITE
RECONNAISSANCE DIVISION

THE BRIDE'S SECRETS

Available August 2009 from Harlequin Intrigue®.

The dark figures on the dock were still firing. The bullets cutting through the surface of the water without the warning boom of shots told Eve they were using silencers.

That was to her benefit. Silencers decreased the accuracy of every shot and lessened the range.

She grabbed for the rocks. Scrambled through the darkness. Bumped her knee on a boulder. Cursed.

Burrowing into the waist-deep grass, she kept low and crawled forward. Faster. Pushed harder. Needed as much distance as possible.

Shots pinged on the rocks.

J.T. scrambled alongside her.

He was breathing hard.

They had to stay close to the ground until they reached the next row of warehouses. Even though she was relatively certain they were out of range at this point, she wasn't taking any risks. And she wasn't slowing down.

J.T. had to keep up.

The splat of a bullet hitting the ground next to Eve had her rolling left. Maybe they weren't completely out of range.

She bumped J.T. He grunted.

His injured arm. Dammit. She could apologize later.

Half a dozen more yards.

Almost in the clear.

As she reached the cover of the alley between the first two warehouses she tensed.

Silence.

No pings or splats.

She glanced back at the dock. Deserted.

Time to run.

Her car was parked another block down.

Pushing to her feet, she sprinted forward. The wet bag dragged at her shoulder. She ignored it.

By the time she reached the lot where her car was parked, she had dug the keys from her pocket and hit the fob. Six seconds later she was behind the wheel. She hit the ignition as J.T. collapsed into the passenger seat. Tires squealed as she spun out of the slot.

"What the hell did you do to me?"

From the corner of her eye she watched him shake his head in an attempt to clear it.

He would be pissed when she told him about the tranquilizer.

She'd needed him cooperative until she formulated a plan. A drug-induced state of unconsciousness had been the fastest and most efficient method to ensure his continued solidarity.

"I can't really talk right now." Eve weaved into the right lane as the street widened to four lanes. What she needed was traffic. It was Saturday night—shouldn't be that difficult to find as soon as they were out of the old warehouse district.

A glance in the rearview mirror warned that their unwanted company had caught up.

Sensing her tension, J.T. turned to peer over his left shoulder.

"I hope you have a plan B."

She shot him a look. "There's always plan G." Then she pulled the Glock out of her waistband.

Cutting the steering wheel left, she slid between two vehicles. Another veer to the right and she'd put several cars between hers and the enemy.

She was betting they wouldn't pull out the firepower in the open like this, but a girl could never be too sure when it came to an unknown enemy.

Deep blending was the way to go.

Two traffic lights ahead the marquis of a movie theater provided exactly the opportunity she was looking for.

The digital numbers on the dash indicated it was just past midnight. Perfect timing. The late movie would be purging its audience into the crowd of teenagers who liked hanging out in the parking lot.

She took a hard right onto the property that sported a twelve-screen theater, numerous fast-food hot spots and a chain superstore. Speeding across the lot, she selected a lane of parking slots. Pulling in as close to the theater entrance as possible, she shut off the engine and reached for her door.

"Let's go."

Thankfully he didn't argue.

Rounding the hood of her car, she shoved the Glock

into her bag, then wrapped her arm around J.T.'s and merged into the crowd.

With her free hand she finger-combed her long hair. It was soaked, as were her clothes. The kids she bumped into noticed, gave her death-ray glares.

They just didn't know.

As she and J.T. moved in closer to the building, she grabbed a baseball cap from an innocent bystander. The crowd made it easy. The kid who owned the cap had made it even easier by stuffing the cap bill-first into his waistband at the small of his back.

Pushing through the loitering crowd, she made her way to the side of the building next to the main entrance. She pushed J.T. against the wall and dropped her bag to the ground. Peeled off her tee and let it fall.

His gaze instantly zeroed in on her breasts, where the cami she wore had glued to her skin like an extra layer. A zing of desire shot through her veins.

Not the time.

With a flick of her wrist she twisted her hair up and clamped the cap atop the blonde mass.

"They're coming," J.T. muttered as he gazed at some point beyond her.

"Yeah, I know." She planted her palms against the wall on either side of him and leaned in. "Keep your eyes open. Let me know when they're inside."

Then she planted her lips on his.

* * * * *

Will J.T. and Eve be caught in the moment?
Or will Eve get the chance to
reveal all of her secrets?
Find out in
THE BRIDE'S SECRETS
by Debra Webb
Available August 2009 from Harlequin Intrigue®.

We'll be spotlighting a different series every month
throughout 2009 to celebrate our 60th anniversary.

LOOK FOR
HARLEQUIN INTRIGUE®
IN AUGUST!

To commemorate the event, Harlequin Intrigue® is thrilled
to invite you to the wedding of the Colby Agency's
J.T. Baxley and his bride, Eve Mattson.

Look for *Colby Agency: Elite Reconnaissance*

THE BRIDE'S SECRETS
BY DEBRA WEBB

Available August 2009

www.eHarlequin.com

Welcome to the intensely emotional world of

MARGARET WAY

with

Cattle Baron: Nanny Needed

It's a media scandal! Flame-haired beauty
Amber Wyatt has gate-crashed her ex-fiancé's
glamorous society wedding. Groomsman
Cal McFarlane knows she's trouble, but when
Amber loses her job, the rugged cattle rancher
comes to the rescue. He needs a nanny, and
if it makes his baby nephew happy, he's
willing to play with fire....

*Available in August
wherever books are sold.*

HRI7601

REQUEST YOUR FREE BOOKS!

2 FREE NOVELS PLUS 2 FREE GIFTS!

HARLEQUIN®

Super Romance®

Exciting, emotional, unexpected!

YES! Please send me 2 FREE Harlequin® Superromance® novels and my 2 FREE gifts (gifts are worth about $10). After receiving them, if I don't wish to receive any more books, I can return the shipping statement marked "cancel." If I don't cancel, I will receive 6 brand-new novels every month and be billed just $4.69 per book in the U.S. or $5.24 per book in Canada. That's a savings of close to 15% off the cover price! It's quite a bargain! Shipping and handling is just 50¢ per book*. I understand that accepting the 2 free books and gifts places me under no obligation to buy anything. I can always return a shipment and cancel at any time. Even if I never buy another book from Harlequin, the two free books and gifts are mine to keep forever.

135 HDN EYLG   336 HDN EYLS

Name	(PLEASE PRINT)
Address	Apt. #
City	State/Prov. Zip/Postal Code

Signature (if under 18, a parent or guardian must sign)

Mail to the **Harlequin Reader Service:**
IN U.S.A.: P.O. Box 1867, Buffalo, NY 14240-1867
IN CANADA: P.O. Box 609, Fort Erie, Ontario L2A 5X3

Not valid to current subscribers of Harlequin Superromance books.

**Are you a current subscriber of Harlequin Superromance books
and want to receive the larger-print edition?
Call 1-800-873-8635 today!**

* Terms and prices subject to change without notice. Prices do not include applicable taxes. Sales tax applicable in N.Y. Canadian residents will be charged applicable provincial taxes and GST. Offer not valid in Quebec. This offer is limited to one order per household. All orders subject to approval. Credit or debit balances in a customer's account(s) may be offset by any other outstanding balance owed by or to the customer. Please allow 4 to 6 weeks for delivery. Offer available while quantities last.

Your Privacy: Harlequin is committed to protecting your privacy. Our Privacy Policy is available online at www.eHarlequin.com or upon request from the Reader Service. From time to time we make our lists of customers available to reputable third parties who may have a product or service of interest to you. If you would prefer we not share your name and address, please check here. ☐

HSR09R

You're invited to join our Tell Harlequin Reader Panel!

By joining our new reader panel you will:

- Receive Harlequin® books—they are FREE and yours to keep with no obligation to purchase anything!
- Participate in fun online surveys
- Exchange opinions and ideas with women just like you
- Have a say in our new book ideas and help us publish the best in women's fiction

In addition, you will have a chance to win great prizes and receive special gifts!
See Web site for details. Some conditions apply.
Space is limited.

To join, visit us at
www.TellHarlequin.com.